STORIA 3
CONSEQUENCES

STORIA 3
CONSEQUENCES

PANDORA

LONDON SYDNEY WELLINGTON

First published by Pandora Press, an imprint of the Trade Division
of Unwin Hyman Limited in 1989.

Pandora Press
Unwin Hyman Limited
15/17 Broadwick Street,
London W1V 1FP

Allen & Unwin Australia Pty Ltd
P. O. Box 764, 8 Napier Street, North Sydney, NSW 2060, Australia

Allen & Unwin New Zealand Pty Ltd with the Port Nicholson Press
Compusales Building, 75 Ghuznee Street, Wellington, New Zealand

Set in Linotron Bembo by Input Typesetting, London

British Library Cataloguing in Publication Data

Storia –III–
  1. Short stories in English. Women writers,
  1945– — Anthologies
823'.01'089287 [FS]

ISBN 0–04–440451–4

Printed in Finland by Werner Söderström Oy

CONTENTS

The Lives of Saints

JEANETTE WINTERSON

Born in 1959, Jeanette Winterson grew up in Lancashire. She now lives and works in London. *Oranges Are Not the Only Fruit* won the 1985 Whitbread Award for a First Novel and is to be televised by the BBC in 1990. *The Passion* was published by Bloomsbury Publishing in 1987 and by Penguin in 1988 and won the John Llewellyn Rhys Prize. Her next novel, *Sexing the Cherry*, is published by Bloomsbury in autumn 1989.

THE LIVES OF SAINTS

That day we saw three Jews in full-length black coats and black hats standing on identical stools looking into the funnel of a pasta machine. One stepped down from his little stool and went to the front where the pasta was stretching out in orange strands. He took two strands and held them up high so that they dropped against his coat. He looked like he'd been decorated with medal ribbon.

They bought the machine. The Italian boys in T-shirts carried it to the truck. They bought the machine because they wanted to make pasta like ringlets to sell in their shop. Their shop sold sacred food and the blinds were always half drawn. The floor was just floorboard, not polished, and the glass counter stood chest high. They served together in their hats and coats. They wrapped things in greaseproof paper. They did this every day except Saturday and after the machine came they made pasta too. They lined the top of the glass counter with wooden trays and they lined the wooden trays with greaseproof paper. Then they laid out the ringlets of fusili in colours they liked, liking orange best in memory of the first day. The shop was dark but for the pasta that glowed and sang from the machine.

It is true that on bright days we are happy. This is true

because the sun on the eyelids effects a chemical change in the body. The sun also diminishes the pupils to pinpricks, letting the light in less. When we can hardly see we are most likely to fall in love. Nothing is commoner in summer than love and I hesitate to tell you of the commonplace but I have only one story and this is it.

In the shop where the Jews stood in stone relief like Shadrach, Meshach and Abednego in the fiery furnace there was a woman who liked to do her shopping in 4 ozs. Even the pasta that fell from the scales in flaming waterfalls trickled into her bag. I was always behind her, coming in from the hot streets to the cool dark that hit like a church. What did she do with her tiny parcels laid in lines on the glass top? Before she paid for them, she always counted them, if there were not sixteen she asked for something else and if there were more than sixteen she had a thing taken away.

I began following her. To begin with I followed just a little way, then, as my obsession grew, I followed in ever-increasing circles from the shop to her home, through the park past the hospital. I lost all sense of time and space and sometimes it seemed to me that I was in the desert or the jungle and still following. Sometimes we were aboriginal in our arcane pathways and other times we walked one street.

I say we. She was oblivious to me. To begin with I kept a respectful distance. I walked on the other side of the road. Then because she never noticed, I got closer and closer, close enough to see that she coloured her hair. The shade was not constant. One day her skirt had a hanging thread and I cut it off without disturbing her. At last I started to walk beside her. We fell in step without the least difficulty. And still she gave no sign of my presence. I began to wonder about myself and took to carrying a mirror to see if I was still there. So far we had walked side by side in silence. Eventually I said, 'Did you know that parrots are left-handed? This is very rare in the animal kingdom. Most creatures are right-handed like us.'

She said nothing and I dredged my mind for things that might please her.

From that day I told her everything I knew. The origin of The Magic Carpet, the nature of cities that last only one day and disappear at nightfall, the register of notes available to a frog during courtship and every story I could remember, including the shortest story in the world. It is by a Guatamalan writer called Augusto Monterroso, 'Cuando desperto, el dinosauro todavia estaba alli'. (When I woke up, the dinosaur was still there.)

Just as Scheherazade prevented her death so I prolonged our life together with my stories. I bound us head-to-foot in words.

Nothing I said had any effect. I felt like Marco Polo who criss-crossed the world searching for a single treasure to please Kublai Khan. The Great Khan was not interested in the Silk Road or the cedar forests he owned. Rich beyond measure he desired something he could not possess. Only one thing could please him and he did not know what that thing was. Polo brought home intricate and fabulous toys and shamans who could teach the emperor how to fly. But when the emperor died, old and exhausted, he knew the world had eluded him.

I rummaged through the out-of-print sections in second-hand bookshops and spent all my spare time in the library. I learned astronomy and mathematics and studied the drawings of Leonardo da Vinci in order to explain how a watermill worked. I was so impatient to tell her all I had discovered that I started waiting for her outside her house. Eventually I knocked on the door at 7 a.m. sharp every morning after that. She was always ready. In winter she carried a torch.

After a few months we were spending the whole of each day together. I made sandwiches for our lunch. She never questioned my choice of filling though I noticed she usually threw away the ones with sardine.

St Teresa of Avila: 'I have no defence against affection. I could be bribed with a sardine.'

So it is with me for whom kindness has always been a surprise. In the lives of saints I look for confirmation of excess. To them it is not strange to spend the nights on a mountain or to forgo food. For them the visionary and the everyday coincide. Above all they have no domestic virtues, preferring intensity to comfort. Despite their inhospitable ways they ferment with unexpected life like those bleak railway cuttings that host horizontal dandelions. They know there is no passion without pain.

As I told her this as I had told her so many things, she turned to me and said, 'Sixteen years ago I lived in a hot country with my husband who was important. We had servants and three children. There was a young man who worked for us. I used to watch his body through the window. In the house we lived such clean lives, always washed and talcumed against the sweat. Not the heat of the day nor the heavy night could unsettle us. We knew how to dress. One evening when the boards were creaking with the weather he came to us where we sat eating small biscuits and dropped two baskets of limes on the floor. He was so tired that he spilt the baskets and went on his knees under my husband's feet. I looked down and saw my husband's black socks within his black shoes. His toe kicked at a lime. I ducked under the table collecting what I could and I could smell the young man smelling

5

of the day and the sun. My husband crossed his legs and I heard him say, "No need for that, Jane."

'Later, when we put out the lamps and I went to my room and Stephen went to his, my armpits were wet and my face looked as though I'd been drinking. I knew he'd come. I took my nightgown off and on four or five times wondering how to greet him. It didn't matter. Not then or afterwards. Not any of the two months that followed. My heart swelled. I had a whale's heart. The arteries of a whale's heart are so wide that a child could crawl through. I found I was pregnant.

'On the night I told him he told me he had to go away. He asked me to go with him and I looked at the verandah and the lamps and Stephen's door that was closed and the children's door that was slightly ajar. I looked at his body. I said I had to stay and he put his head on my stomach and cried. On the day he left I lay in my room and when I heard his flight coming over the house I wrapped my head in a towel. Stephen opened the door and said, "Are you staying?" I said I was. He said, "Never mention this again." I never did. Not that or anything else.'

We walked on in silence. We walked through the hours of the day until we arrived at nightfall and came to a castle protected by a moat. Lions guarded the gateway.

'I'm going in now,' she said.

I looked up from my thoughts and saw an ordinary house fronted by a pretty garden and a pair of tabbys washing their paws. Which was the story and which was real? Could it be true that a woman who had not spoken for sixteen years except to order her food was now walking into this small house full of everyday things? Was it not more likely that she would disappear into her magic kingdom and leave me on the other side of the water, my throat clogged with feelings that resist words?

I followed her across the moat and saw our reflections in the water. I wanted to reach down and scoop her in my arms, let her run over my body until both of us were wet through. I wanted to swim inside her. We crossed the moat and she fed me on boiled cabbage. I have heard it is a cure for gout. She never spoke as we ate and afterwards she took a candle and took me upstairs. I was surprised to see a mosquito net in England.

Time is not constant and time in stories least of all. Anyone can fall asleep and lose generations in their dreams. The night I spent with her has taken up my whole life and now I live attached to myself like a codicil. It is not because I lack interests, indeed I have recently reworked Leonardo's drawings and built for myself a very fine watermill. It is simply that being with her allowed me to be myself. There was no need to live normally. Now, I know so many stories and such a collection of strange things and I wonder who would like them since I cannot do them justice on my own. The heart of a whale is the height of a man. . . .

I left her at dawn. The street was quiet, only a cat and the electric whirr of the milk van. I kept looking back at the candle in the window until it was as far away as the faint point of a fading star. In the early sky all the stars had faded by the time I got home. There was the retreating shape of the moon and nothing more.

Every day I went to the shop where the Jews stood in stone relief and I bought things that pleased me. I took my time, time being measured in 4 ozs. She never came in. I waited outside her house for some years until a FOR SALE sign appeared and a neighbour told me the woman next door had vanished. I felt such pleasure then, to know that she was wandering the world and that one day, one day, I might find her again. When I do, all the stories that are folded into this one can be shaken out and let loose. But until then, like the lives of saints, more is contained than can be revealed. The world itself will roll up like a scroll taking time and space away. All stories end here.

A Brave Young Woman

GILLIAN FREEMAN

Gillian Freeman is the author of eleven novels, three non-fiction books and many scripts for radio, television and film. She also wrote the scenarios for two Kenneth MacMillan ballets, *Mayerling* and *Isadora*, for The Royal Ballet. She is married to Edward Thorpe, writer and ballet critic of *The Standard*, with whom she collaborated on *Ballet Genius*, published in 1988. They have two daughters, Harriet and Matilda, both actresses.

A BRAVE YOUNG WOMAN

London Airport
Saturday

Dear Miss Spencer,

My flight home to Australia is delayed and I am writing to you on an impulse I hope you will forgive and understand. I have just read in today's *Express* that during last night's performance of *Swan Lake* you damaged your knee and will not be dancing again for some time.

My sister, Louise Mitchell, who lives in Flat 7, Empress Court, Empress Road, Fulham, is an ardent admirer of yours. Her dream was to become a dancer but unfortunately finance and then ill health prevented her from continuing her ballet lessons. She has a brain tumour and is waiting for an operation.

I am not able to stay in England any longer (I have a young family in Melbourne) but I know it would give her untold pleasure if, during your enforced leisure, you could spare an hour to visit her. The telephone is a communal one for the building, so if you feel you would like to do this, I suggest you write to tell her when it will be convenient for you.

She goes out very seldom and her doctor always comes on Wednesday mornings.

Of course you may have made it a rule to avoid personal contact with your fans. If this is the case I know Louise would be thrilled with a signed photograph with perhaps a special inscription.

I hope your injury is not too severe.

Yours sincerely,

Ruth Church

The letter put my torn ligament into perspective. I had been in a sour mood, depressed and disappointed that I could not guest with the Paris Opera Ballet, would not be able to rehearse the *Petroushka* revival for the Royal Birthday Gala. But what were they compared to the prospect of an operation for a brain tumour? I sent the signed photograph with a letter suggesting I should drop by one afternoon for a cup of tea.

'Are you sure?' asked my husband as he took the envelope to post with his office mail, 'that you want to become involved?'

'I won't become involved,' I said. 'I shan't go again. But I would feel guilty for the rest of my life if I refused.'

Louise did not write back. She telephoned from the hall of Empress Court with its graffiti and worn linoleum tiles which were to become so familiar to me over the next months. Her voice was childishly light and sweet, nervous, excited and hesitant as she thanked me for the letter and photograph and excused her sister for the imposition of even suggesting a meeting. 'But it would be wonderful to actually talk to you about . . . well *everything*. I'm alone so much and now Ruth has gone back . . . she just came for Easter, we thought she'd be here for my operation

11

but they postponed it. I only see the social worker and she doesn't even know what ballet *is*!'

The voice had given me a visual image of someone slight and frail like the dance students I sometimes take for class, like the students we were ourselves, slender, straight-backed, with that distinctive turned-out walk. When I climbed the dark stairs for the first time and rang the bell of Number 7 I was not prepared for the obese young woman who confronted me. I thought she was the social worker. I said, 'I've come to see Louise . . .'

'*I'm* Louise.' She held out her hands and I found myself extending mine for her to draw me over the threshold. 'I know you expected . . .' she looked down at her tent of a dress and laughed a little with no hint of self-pity '. . . because I said I'd danced. It's the drugs I have to take. It's no good being vain. Don't smile, but I still do a kind of *barre*, the back of the bedroom chair. But not in front of a mirror!'

The front door opened directly into the living room, and although the entrance and stairwell were dirty and shabby, Louise's flat was clean and bright with a nursery atmosphere, pale pink walls, framed prints of baby animals, patchwork cushions. Tea was set out on a white table-cloth and the white iced cake was decorated with smarties. There were sandwiches, too, cut into triangles with the crusts cut off. The paper napkins were the same shade of pink as the lines which decorated the rims of the cups and the edges of the plates.

'You've gone to so much trouble!'

'I'm so thrilled to have a visitor. I'm afraid I made the cake from a packet.'

'I *always* make cakes from packets!'

'If you ice them nobody knows.'

'Unless you tell them, Louise!'

There was no doubt that we had rapport. We talked freely, soon leaving the jokey *badinage* for her background and family and my dancing career. Occasionally she referred to her terrible predicament, but always in a matter-of-fact manner when it was relevant to whatever was under discussion. My heart ached for her, the near poverty which she had made such effort to disguise, the loneliness, the damaged hopes and the physical ugliness. I don't mean that her features were not pretty, one could see that she once had been, but her complexion was grey, her hair lustreless and not even the loose patterned dress could conceal the body that no circus strongman, let alone a dancer (and she talked with shining eyes of Nureyev) could have lifted.

At half-past five she suddenly looked at her watch and asked me to go. 'This is so embarrassing. I feel awful. But my social worker, Mrs Trevor . . . on Tuesday evenings she always comes to wash my hair. . . .'

'Of course. You don't have to explain. I have to go now anyway.'

'It's so good of her to come that I wouldn't want her to feel she was interrupting anything.'

'Louise, I understand. And you can reward her with a slice of that delicious packet cake!'

'I have so enjoyed myself, Veronica.'

'So have I.'

'Is there any chance . . . I know I shouldn't even be asking you. . . .'

'I'd love to come again. Next time I won't make it a Tuesday.'

'Wednesday? The doctor gives me my injection on Wednesdays and it would be something to look forward to.'

'Then I shall be here on Wednesday.'

'Will you come for lunch?'

'Only if you allow me to bring it.'

Reluctantly she agreed, assuring me that she could arrange for Mrs Trevor to shop, would have time to prepare it, and then gracefully giving way to my persuasion, with the charm and tact she brought to everything so that neither of us should feel uncomfortable although we both knew that money was tight for her.

I talked about her to Tim, not only during the evening, but as we lay in bed.

'I thought you said you weren't going to get involved.'

'The problem is I like her. I really do like her.'

He put his arm round me. 'Don't become too attached.' It was a loving warning. 'She has an uncertain future.'

'Which is why she needs a friend. When you meet her you'll feel the same. I've never met such a brave young woman.'

In the weeks which followed I managed to persuade her to come with me to the local shops to buy food, to choose a new shampoo for the weekly hair-washing marathon.

'Poor Mrs Trevor. She doesn't think beyond cleanliness. She is *not* an imaginative shopper.' This went for everything Louise asked her to buy, the list adhered to but in the most perfunctory way. I was horrified by Louise's diet of pork pies, frozen chips, packets of biscuits, sugar-coated cereals, sliced white bread.

'Louise, you're overweight, you're soon going to have a serious operation. You have to build up your strength with the right foods, be as fit as you possibly can in the circumstances.'

But she was grateful to Mrs Trevor and fearful to go out.

'You won't be alone. I shall be with you.' It was then

that I learned that from time to time, with no warning, she suffered small haemorrhages, bouts of dizziness, loss of vision, was terrified of meeting with an accident.

'I really am afraid, Veronica. I haven't been out for more than a year. When my sister was here we did go to church on Easter Sunday, but we took a taxi and I literally clung to her arm.'

'Cling to my arm. We won't go far. Just to the Fulham Road.'

At last she agreed, holding on to the bannisters with both hands on the way down ('I do this when I go down to telephone!') and then hanging on to me as we made our slow progress along Empress Road. A mild euphoria overcame her in the chemist's as she selected not only shampoo, but a new lipstick and some soap.

'It's like Aladdin's cave. Thank you thank you *thank you* for winning the battle.'

In the grocer's I directed her to muesli and wholemeal bread; at the greengrocer's I bought her imported straw-berries and a melon. As we turned into the doorway of Empress Court she was giggling and joking and I noticed that as we climbed the stairs she held the bannister with one hand.

By now I knew all about her family, the parents who were killed in a train crash in Holland, the aunt, now dead, who had brought her up with her sister Ruth and brother John. John had been the first to go to Australia, living with a woman who had never divorced. Ruth had followed, married 'an Ozzi' and had three children. Louise had been going to Melbourne when the tumour was diag-nosed. She had intended to emigrate. 'I wanted to be with the people I cared about and who cared about me.' Ruth was not happy with her husband but for the children's

15

sake she intended to stay with him. 'We lost our parents, we know what it feels like to be insecure.' I saw photographs of them all, Ruth's wedding, back garden barbecues, school outings. I talked as if I knew them. She read me their letters and when she wrote to Ruth I added a little note to say how much I enjoyed being with Louise.

The ballet was Tim's idea. 'Why don't you invite her to come with us to the Gala?' He hadn't yet met her and I was overwhelmed by his generosity. I had thought he harboured irritation. I knew I talked about Louise too much, but she had become integral to my life. Besides which, the Gala tickets were fifty pounds each; not only was it a Royal birthday but a charity night as well.

'Tim, that is very dear of you.'

'She deserves a special treat. And so do you. You've changed her life. We'll take her to dinner afterwards, somewhere memorable. Maybe the Savoy Grill.'

At first, as I knew she would, Louise demurred. She had not yet gone out at night and her anxiety was physically apparent. For a moment her face lit up with joy, then she began to tremble.

'Ask your doctor.'

'Even if he says yes, I don't have anything to wear.'

'I will buy you something to wear.'

'It will be a disappointing night for you, won't it, Veronica? You were going to dance in *Petroushka*.'

'I'm not disappointed any more, that's history. There'll be other *Petroushkas*. But I will be disappointed if you're not there. Think,' I encouraged her, 'all your idols. On stage or in the audience. Nureyev, Fonteyn. . . .'

'It would be an experience of a lifetime.' She bit her lip suddenly and the word *lifetime* seemed suspended in the air.

16

A second's silence, then I retrieved the tangible present. 'Now, about your dress . . . ?'

She asked me to choose some material for her to make it up at home. She said she could not face the trying on and it would be too much money, but I think we both were daunted at the prospect of an outsize clothes department and the inevitable all round mirrors. She gave me her measurements in metres ('It makes it so much better because I don't know exactly what it means, I still think in yards!') and I bought peacock blue shot silk which looked glorious in quantity. I even managed to get her to the hairdressers, and with her knowledge spoke to the assistant explaining her situation and asking him to be gentle when massaging the scalp. When I collected her, she was glowing, with an ornamental comb holding her shining hair in place, and to me she appeared beautiful in spite of all her shortcomings, an inner radiance I cannot properly describe. The dress she had made on her hand sewing machine had its failings, but Tim shook her hand and told her she looked stunning, and she blushed and beamed and looked at him under lowered lashes like the Princess of Wales.

I watched her almost as much as I watched the stage. She smiled, she gasped, she applauded and she cried. 'It has been the most fantastic night of my whole life.' But as we left our coats in the Savoy cloakroom, she suddenly took my hand in a paroxysm of anxiety and made me promise to watch her over dinner in case she had a dizzy spell.

'I promise.'

'Because I had one yesterday. I didn't dare tell you in case you said I couldn't go.'

'The doctor said you could go.'

'They do, don't they, to make you feel you're normal. . . . Let me sit next to you, Veronica. If I feel it happening I'll press you under the table. No-one else need know there's anything wrong. If you just hold my hand tight. . . .'

She pressed my hand now and I could feel the tension. 'If I pass out, call my doctor.' She opened the little gold bag I had lent her and took out a piece of paper. 'Here is his name and number. . . .'

'It won't happen,' I said. 'Not tonight.'

Louise said with sadness which was not customary. 'Anything can happen at any time. I've grown used to it.'

We were joined by two other dancers from the company, not people I would normally be overjoyed to dine with, but delighted tonight because I knew that for Louise it was the final thrill of the occasion. There were other celebrities in the elegant panelled Grill Room, and I watched her look from one table to another in increasing excitement. Our table companions had performed at the Gala and told inside stories spiced with gossip. Louise was incredulous, enthralled and full of questions. She had forgotten herself, she was like a child. Then, quite unexpectedly, because I had forgotten, too, I felt her hand against my leg under the table, pressing urgently, and I grasped her hand and held it tightly between my own as she whispered, 'I can't see. I can't see. I can't see anything at all.'

Tim scrambled to his feet, came round to support her from behind. The others stood in alarm.

'Call a doctor.'

'There's a name in my purse. . . .'

'It's all right, Louise. Sit tight. You're going to be O.K.'

'I'm sorry,' she managed to say. 'I'm so sorry. . . .'

'Call the doctor for heaven's sake. . . .'

But just as Tim took the piece of paper from my purse, I felt Louise relax and lean against me. 'It's all right. I can see you.' She began to cry.

'Look,' said one of the dancers, 'take her home, take her to a hospital.'

'No,' sobbed Louise. 'I don't need to go anywhere. It's over now. But I've spoiled your evening and you've done so much for me.'

We all comforted her and reassured her. 'All that matters is that you're feeling better.'

'You're very brave.'

'I'm not brave. I'm an emcumbrance. I shall never ever go out at night again.'

'How about a brandy?'

'No, no, she'd better not. . . .'

'Are you allowed to drink, Louise?'

'I'm allowed to eat,' she said with a tearful smile, spirit returning. 'I saw some delicious things go by on the trolley.'

Now we all smiled. 'You shall have everything from the trolley.'

Tim clicked his fingers to the waiter and it was wheeled to Louise's side.

'Charlotte russe, mousse *au chocolat*, fresh raspberries, crème caramel . . .'

'I'd like that one . . . could I have raspberries with it?'

'Of course. The whole bowlful if you feel like it.'

We watched her spooning and eating and licking the cream from her lips as if she were performing a miracle.

Our holiday, Tim's and mine, was approaching. We were going to Venice, our favourite city in the world.

'Send me a postcard, won't you?' said Louise.

'We'll send you several postcards. But they'll probably arrive at least two weeks after we're back.'

I knew she would miss me, but true to character she only expressed pleasure in what I would see and do. She made me promise to keep a diary so that I would not miss any detail on return. 'What you do, what you eat, who you meet. I want to imagine it all. Because I've seen that film with Katherine Hepburn, what's it called? And it looked so incredibly beautiful.'

'It is incredibly beautiful. We did the cliché thing and spent our honeymoon there.'

'If ever I get married that's where I'll spend my honeymoon.' I nodded and smiled as if there were a prospect, but I could not meet her eyes.

It was the night before we left that she telephoned me. I knew before she told me that something had happened to impel her to go downstairs to the hall. 'Veronica. I wouldn't bother you when you're getting ready to go . . . but it really is very very important.'

'I'll come now.'

I left Tim to sit on the cases and took a cab to Empress Road, running up the stairs my heart beating fast. She heard my steps and opened the door before I reached the landing.

'I'm sorry. I'm sorry.'

'What is it, darling? You've really got me scared.'

'There was no-one else to ask.' I followed her into the living room where my own framed photograph now hung among the puppies and kittens on the wall.

We sat down opposite one another. There were two used cups on the table. She saw me register them. 'The doctor was here. . . .'

'I thought he only ever came on Wednesday mornings.'
No doubt I looked as afraid as I felt.

'He came after his surgery. Veronica. It's next week.
My operation is next week.'

'Oh Louise. When I'm away.'

'I'm glad you're going to be away. I wouldn't even
have told you. It's just that . . .' her voice shook slightly.
'If anything, well, happens to me . . . I have to face it.'
She held up her hand to stop my platitudes. 'I've written
some letters, to John and Ruth, and if when you come
back . . . I want you to post them. And there is one for
the children, although it won't mean anything to them
until they're grown up. But Janice already goes to ballet
class, and if . . . if. . . .'

I couldn't speak. I took the three thick envelopes, already stamped for Australia.

'The doctor explained everything to me very honestly.
I may not survive . . . mentally. Not the way I am. Until
they find out just how much they have to take away. . . .'

'You didn't have to put stamps on them.'

'You know I'm too proud!' And we were actually
laughing. Laughing! When we were possibly saying goodbye for ever. 'Enjoy Venice. Enjoy every single second.
Don't think of me. Put me out of your mind. Time
enough when you get home. Promise.'

Venice was perfect, of course, but the squares and alleys
and domes and arches were so incredibly beautiful that
we thought of Louise even more poignantly than if we
had been somewhere mundane. We talked about her as
we lay on the Lido beach under a pink and yellow
umbrella, as we sat by the Grand Canal eating dinner and
watching the moon, as we drank our apéritifs in St Marks
Square while conflicting orchestras played. When we

made love I found myself thinking not of Tim but of an unlovely body in a London hospital bed, head bandaged and God knows what in the mind.

It was ironic that the place we had most wanted to be was now the place we were anxious to leave. As the plane taxied towards the terminal at Heathrow I said, 'I'm going to telephone the doctor from the customs hall,' and I took out the piece of paper I had kept since the traumatic night in the Savoy Grill. But the phones were all in use or out of order and our mounting apprehension shadowed us to our front door.

There was a letter on the mat, pushed through the box and marked personal, and I recognised Louise's writing as I picked it up, tore it open and flooded with relief.

Dearest Veronica and Tim
I am going to be very brave and deliver this myself to save you a moment's worry. My operation was postponed again at the eleventh hour. I don't know whether I am pleased or sorry. So I am at home and when you have unpacked and slept and done all the things which I'm sure will have piled up in your absence, please bring the photographs round to Empress Court.
Love from Louise.

It was on a Wednesday, the doctor's injection day, that Louise asked me if she could go with me to Cumbria, my annual week of dog-sitting for the ballet teacher who had recognised my potential in a class of six-year-olds all those years ago. Dog-sitting was small return for having been put in the path of a career. I had told Louise about her, the Russian who ended up in Keswick after glory with the Ballet Russe, about the cottage furnished in the grand style and the Scots terrier called Burns.

'I know I shouldn't ask, but may I come with you?' There was an underlying desperation in the voice that made me answer her question with another.

'Did the doctor give you a date for the operation?'

She said bleakly, 'How did you know?'

'Because I can think of no other reason you would even consider it.'

'You mustn't be angry, Veronica. I asked the doctor. He said he would give me one of those filled hypodermics just in case I had one of my special turns!' She went to the window and spoke with her back to me. I wondered if she saw the slated roof tops and the cinema cupola with its neon sign. 'It may be my last chance to be normal. To have an ordinary holiday like other people. You'll go back there next year, the year after. You'll go to Venice again, and Paris and New York. But I may be a vegetable or I may be dead. I want to go for walks with that dog. I want to look at the lakes and mountains and eat bread from the little baker's shop you've told me about and see the different way they slice bacon . . . see for *myself*, not just hear about it. I want to see the icon over the old oak beams!'

I said hesitantly, 'I'd be afraid.'

'If I die,' she said passionately, 'I'd rather die there, with a friend, than on an operating table or in a ward. Please take me. Please let me have that one free, happy week.'

'Of course I'll take you,' I said. 'Anyway, it will be far nicer being there with you than on my own.'

Tim was aghast. 'You must be mad. It's all very well for

23

her to talk about wanting to die there. A nice romantic concept. But the reality is fraught. It's moral blackmail.'

'I couldn't say no.'

'Then for heaven's sake talk to her doctor, make sure he really agrees. Be prepared, at least have him write a letter in case you have to call an ambulance.' He paused. 'I don't like it. I don't like it. God, you've never given an injection in your life. You're squeamish enough when someone injects you.'

'All right,' I said. 'I'll speak to the doctor, I'll go by what he says. But I cannot leave her behind.'

In the morning I telephoned the receptionist and asked for an appointment. 'I want to discuss a patient. I'm not asking him to be unethical. It is Louise Mitchell so I'm sure he'll understand. I am taking her on holiday before she goes into hospital for her operation.'

'Louise Mitchell,' said the receptionist. 'The name doesn't ring a bell. Please hold on a moment.' After a full minute she returned to me. 'I'm sorry, I think you must have the wrong doctor. I can't see a Louise Mitchell on the files here. Perhaps you're mixing up Dr Walker with Dr Warner in Walton Street. It happens all the time.'

'Look,' I said exasperated, 'Louise gave me this number herself. He visits her every Wednesday. She has a brain tumour and she is being operated on in two weeks time. It is essential I speak to the doctor in case there is an emergency when we're away.'

She said, 'Please hold on again. I'll have a word with him.' When she came back she said, 'I'm sorry, I have found her card. Dr Walker will see you at the end of surgery this afternoon.'

I felt I knew Dr Walker, just as I knew Ruth and John,

because we had talked about him so often. I knew he was not always outwardly sympathetic, but Louise said that his brusque manner gave her the strength to face her ordeal because he spoke positively. He did not conceal possibilities but he was always optimistic. I had imagined a blunt, handsome Scot. At some time or another she must have said something about his Edinburgh accent, so I was taken aback by the small, balding Englishman who wore his old school tie.

'Do please sit down.' He was quiet, uncharismatic and gentle. 'I think there was some confusion this morning when you spoke to my secretary. You were asking about Louise Mitchell, I understand.'

I launched into my story again, that I wanted to take her away for a short holiday before she went into hospital, but that I did not want to be unprepared. I told him about the episode at the restaurant table, but explained that Louise had confidence in me, that I was the only person she trusted to accompany her out of doors.

'There does seem to be a misunderstanding,' he said, looking at a card on the desk before him. 'My secretary has only been here two years which is why she did not recall Miss Mitchell.'

'Well of course,' I said, 'she doesn't come *here*.'

'No indeed,' said Dr Walker. 'Nor do I go there, wherever *there* is. Is it still Empress Court?' He glanced again at the card. 'That is the address she gave when she registered with me five years ago. I only saw her that once. She asked for some sleeping pills. I prescribed Mogadon. I did make a note here that she was very overweight. If she had come back at any time I would have suggested she had a blood test.'

I said, 'She has an injection every Wednesday morning. You go. . . .'

'On Wednesday mornings,' he said, 'I am at my pre-
natal clinic. I think,' and he rose to his feet indicating that
our meeting was over, 'that you would be unwise to
allow Miss Mitchell to accompany you to the country or
anywhere else.'

I could not contain myself, the anger, the disappointment,
the bitterness of having been cheated, my foolishness at
having been so gullibly blind. I went straight round to
Empress Court and as soon as Louise had closed the door,
I said, 'You lied. You lied from the start. I've seen your
doctor. How dare you. How dare you.' To my horror
she struck me across the cheek.

'You've been spying on me,' she screamed, thrusting
me back against the wall. 'I really trusted you. I thought
you were honest. Oh, you think you've got everything,
don't you? Looks, a husband, career . . . and now you
want to spoil my one chance of a holiday. One week.
How do you think it feels to live here? My only family
in Australia. I suppose you begrudge the time you've
spent with me. The money you've spent on me. Is that
what you think of me? A fat, ugly, stupid woman?'

'Not stupid,' I said, wresting myself free and getting
to the door as fast as I could. 'Not stupid at all. Manipulat-
ing, deceitful and clever.' And I slammed the door behind
me and, really crying now, ran down the stairs.

The letters she had given me to post before Venice were
still in the kitchen drawer. As soon as I reached home I
opened them. The pages were blank of course.

And that, I thought, was the end of it, except that I
went through what seemed like a period of mourning, as
if I had experienced a death. For weeks I did not sleep
without waking and thinking of her, reliving the humili-

ation, the sense of betrayal. I talked about her, I dreamt about her, and if she had obsessed me before when I believed her, now her duplicity dominated my life. It was two years before I was able to tell the story at dinner parties without a twisting in my heart. I avoided the area around Empress Road, sickeningly afraid that we might meet. But at last I recovered and the episode took its place among other memories, incapable of damaging me more. Until, that is, last summer, when Magda came to play at Wimbledon and lost the Ladies Singles by a point.

Afterwards she stayed on in London, and we spent several days together, shopping, lunching, going to plays. One wet July afternoon we had planned to – she's American – 'do a movie' but she rang me to say she had to call it off.

'I hate to do this to you at the last minute,' she apologised, 'but something has cropped up that I cannot get out of. I'm on an errand of mercy.'

'What kind of errand of mercy?' It was almost as if I knew.

'Well, I had a letter,' said Magda, 'from a Canadian woman. She'd posted it at the airport on her way home. She'd read in the papers that I was still here for the charity tournament, and she has this sister, a poor kid who was a terrific tennis player, waiting for a brain tumour to be removed. She asked if I would go visit her. I mean, we can see the movie another time. This is one of the days the doctor doesn't visit and I'd be pretty despicable if I refused.'

For the record we saw the film, but I felt inexplicitly guilty, as if I were the one who had betrayed a friend.

Mostly Southend

MAGGIE HEMINGWAY

Maggie Hemingway was born in Orford, Suffolk. After an early childhood spent in New Zealand she returned to England and now divides her time between London and the Kent coast. She worked for some years in publishing before becoming a full-time writer. *The Bridge* was published in 1986 to considerable acclaim and won the Royal Society of Literature's Winifred Holtby Prize. This was followed in 1988 by *Stop House Blues*, hailed by the *Times Literary Supplement* as 'a *tour de force* of the imagination with no obvious antecedents'.

MOSTLY SOUTHEND

Sometimes I think my life is all waiting. I wait, and beyond me I can hear the blur of others enmeshed in their lives: explosions of joy and sinuous repetitions of deceit. But where I am is timeless, sightless, soundless almost. Speechless. I've come to know it well. It's not a place in which I live, exactly. Not *live* in the vital sense of the word, but to which I *return*. Not voluntarily. Oh no, I wouldn't have you think that. I don't do nothing voluntarily. It's where you get put – to wait. Between assignments. Or when you're not needed on a long job. They like to keep us separate. They won't have no fraternising, not on the job; nor off it, either. They like to know exactly where we are at any time, they've always got their eye on us, a part of their brain watching us, even when we're asleep; listening, probably, even to our breathing. We're their property, you see, that's how they regard us. Blooming nerve I say, but not out loud.

If I had to choose between the long and the short I'd pick the short. 'Cause the funny thing is, I've noticed, they often don't plan the short assignment as well as they do the long. I suppose they think: send us in, do the job, and pull us out again, quick. Whereas on the long they work it out to the last detail, every alibi watertight, every

moment accounted for, no slipping off for a quick fag,
no freelancing, no chance to do it your own way. No
chance, ever, to do it your own way. That's the last thing
they want. Mess it all up that would, so they think. That's
why you don't get told anything till the last moment; not
where you're going or who you'll be – 'cover' we call it
in the trade – or how many others are in on the job. Not
how dangerous, 'course they wouldn't tell you that. Or
how boring. There's a lot of boredom, lot of sitting round
waiting, like now. Marking time. First thing you see,
generally, are your clothes; different set for each assignment. That's the first hint you get of what's coming.
That's when you know, when your heart sinks. Or tigh-
tens with excitement – you catch your breath, you
wonder. Sinks mostly. You get a stained tie and a pair of
worn flannels, you ain't going to no Savoy. No. Southend
if you're lucky. My life's been mostly Southend. And
abroad. I get abroad now and then. Used to get a real thrill
travelling to the airport in the early morning. There's
something about early morning airports. You leave the
sleeping city and you go out, through the silence, to this
waiting place. The empty lounges, the deceptive, dozy
quiet, the cleaners sleepwalking with soft brooms, and
beyond the heavy glass the planes roaring noiselessly out
on the tarmac. The sense of it all coming together: a new
place, a new day, a new beginning. But it's always the
same scruffy flannels and it's always the back streets of
Budapest or the waterfront at Tangiers. I was ill for a
week there, once, really bad, something I ate, had to keep
on working, though, all through it. Could've died. But
I suppose it wasn't in their plan.

I fancy Madagascar. It said in a book I read once: the
shape of Madagascar is never constant. As you approach

it from the sea, whatever time of day, you cannot see its outline. Under the mist of dawn it slips away on either side into the waves, and in the juddering haze of midday it dissolves, streaming upwards into a sky liquid with heat. At night, crossing the inky blackness of the strait, the lights of the port dance in the water. The scent of it floats across the darkness. You think that you come closer and closer; you anticipate the grate of the boat's prow on the jetty, feel the warm stone under your hand, but the lights dance away. You sail on through the oily lap of water and the rush of stars, and before you Madagascar recedes and advances, withdrawing all sense of time. The journey that you thought would take minutes seems to lengthen into hours and weeks and years. I'd like that. I'd like Madagascar. In Madagascar I could be whatever I wanted. I'd be free at last. If Madagascar has no shape then neither would I, at least not one of theirs; I'd devise one of my own. I've been doing that anyway, in secret. In between. We aren't supposed to do anything in between; we have to lay low. They'd like us not to bre- athe, not to think, not exist, probably. Not think, especially. But I have – been thinking. They think we can't, until they give us something to think about. But I've been practising, I've been going on 'in the mode' as it were, after an assignment's over. Each time I manage to keep it going for longer. I have to be careful, though, they don't find out. Criminal, isn't it, that you don't get no life of your own, you can't never choose. Nobody knows ourselves better than we do, we should be the ones deciding what we're going to be. But no, you just take what you're given and you're supposed to be grateful. And we all are. Oh, thank you ma'am, Cyril Biggs insurance claims inspector, disenchanted wife, two sullen kids, a terrace in Morplugia Drive with an outside lav.

31

Oh, yes, that's just what I wanted. Make you laugh if it didn't make you cry. But I never heard no-one refuse a life. It's just not done. Why not, I want to know. Why *not*?

I been sitting thinking, in this grey place. And what I come to was – well, why don't we form a union? Air our grievances. Take a stand, together. They'd be forced to listen to our demands then, wouldn't they? Give us our own lives. One by one they can pick us off, that's what everyone's afraid of. And it happens. There *are* them who take a stand. They don't refuse exactly, they don't talk back, I never heard of no-one doing that, but they go sulky on the job. They stonewall, they won't interact properly. 'Course, generally, *they* can get round them one way or another, circumvent them. *They* got all kinds of tricks. But if they can't circumvent them, if they can't – well, they just eliminate them. You never see them again. They don't even get a bit part in future assignments. We're all afraid of that, of not coming back. If we got together, though . . . They couldn't wipe us out and start again with all new people. Be far too much bother. I mean we're professionals; be ages before they could work up replacements for us. You can give us any role at a moment's notice and we take it on and no-one can tell we've been there before in a different hat and a squeaky voice. No, they'd never do it. Trouble is, they keep us all apart. We're never allowed to get together except on assignment and then we're not supposed to talk apart from what we're meant to say. We don't even get tea-breaks – well, you don't in a life, do you – so how on earth would we organise a union meeting? And another thing, what would we call it? You can't have a union with no name. I've sat here, in this grey whirling-dervish emptiness of a place, and I've thought and I've thought, as much as I can, but nothing won't come to mind. Nothing right. And it's got to be right. That's one thing about this business. The words. Sometimes I think it's the only good thing about it. They can be a real treat, the words, real classy. Except when they're slipshod. And then we wince; goes right through you, really hurts. It can knock years off you, a bad assignment like that. If they can't do it properly, I say, they should leave it to us; we all know what we'd like to be, we all know what we do best.

I've never had my full potential realised. Never. Not once. They've never understood me. Got me right. All they give me is the same lives over and over again. And I haven't wanted none of them. It drives you desperate, turns you mad. Makes you despair. But even mad would be better than what I get – be more interesting. I'd give anything for an interesting life. Anything! I'm willing, I'm able, and what do I get? I get the thinning hair and the ugly wife, and feet that bulge out of shoes that are always dull with the dust of mean streets. I get the little-man lives. I carry the parcels and pass the assassin the gun. But I aspire to higher things. And I've realised, I've come to see, that the only way is to go and get them for myself. Next time they hand me out another life I don't want I'm going to be ready with one of my own. I got it all worked out. I saw this guy once, on an assignment somewhere; he passed me in the street, that was all, but I never forgot him. That's him! I said to myself. That's the real me! I tell you – little black moustache, proper haircut, snappy dresser, two-tone shoes in real leather; hadn't got much of a chin but it made him look kind of aristocratic. Snapped his fingers and got in a cab. Well! I thought, well, that's me. I been practising him ever since, when I can, and I got him down to a T. Cyril Biggs? Not a chance! Not any more. I've always been docile. Well that's over! I'm going to have the other life. I am, I'm determined. I'm going to do it. Very next novel I'm in. Soon as I feel the kind of shifting, swirling movement that always comes when the grey starts blowing apart and separating out into lines – unwrapping we call it in the trade, pulling the wool off our eyes – I'll be ready. And things are going to start up again soon, I can sense it. They keep us in a sort of timelessness so we can't guess anything, so we can't anticipate and get ideas of our own. But we're not so daft as they think. If you're a pro then you can sense things changing, you become aware of their mind moving onto you. Like a vibration in the air, it is; an increase in the electrical charge same as before a thunderstorm, only ten times worse. You start feeling a bit queasy, like your balance was upset. And the pain! Every time I think I can't stand it. The air rushing into your lungs. Terrible! Drowning and gasping, you'd think it was death not life! And the blood shooting down your veins pushing and stretching. You'd never think tube walls could be stretched like that, you think they're going to split. And the ache! Worse than sciatica it is. And then, and then, in all the gasping and roaring you hear this faint rasping, like a rasp and a breath all in one, a quick light shushing sound. And you know that's it. That's the page turning. Everything goes brilliant white, no grey no more, all the searchlights turned on piercing white, and lower and lower comes the black shadow, the nib pointing straight at your heart. Oh my Gawd, what am I talking about! What am I doing talking and not watching. Can't you see it? The grey dancing in wavy lines, getting lighter and . . . I can't breathe, I can't breathe, I can't. . . . Where is he? Where's the – I got him – little moustache, parted hair. . . . Hold on! Snap your fingers, snap . . . Goodbye Cyril, I'm going in my own life. I got my own . . . There's a cuff coming round my wrist. Now we'll see, now we'll . . . Here! There's a spot! On the cuff. There's a fray round the button! Hey! You give me the wrong shirt. It's wrong! I'm not having this one – I'm not! I got something else in mind. I got a better idea. Listen! *Listen*. . . .

Cyril Biggs ran the last fifty yards from Morplugia Drive with a curious paddling run designed to move his legs while keeping his upper body inert. But even so he missed the green light on the pedestrian crossing by several seconds.

'Wait for the little green man,' he whispered to himself and tried to remember the joke the traveller with Rawsons had told him yesterday about little green men. A crowd began to gather around him, all staring with early morning blankness at the tube station in front of them across the road. A girl pushed in beside Cyril's right shoulder. He glanced at her and quickly looked away again, patting cautiously at the strands of hair stuck across the crown of his head, fingering them one by one. The light changed and they all surged across.

'Fulham Broadway,' said Cyril to the ticket clerk.

His first visit that morning was to investigate an insurance claim on three new pasta machines at Moses Brothers in the Empress Road. Keeping the coins the clerk gave back to him ready in his hand, he allowed himself to be borne on one of the jostling currents of people through the booking hall towards the newspaper stand.

'Never mention this again,' snapped a man to his right.

'She has an injection every Wednesday morning,' said a woman just behind him.

'Give us a *Sun*, Fred,' Cyril winked. 'For a change.'

Relative Values

EVA FIGES

Eva Figes was born in Berlin and came to England in 1939. Her second novel *Winter Journey* (1967) won The Guardian Fiction Prize. She is the author of ten novels including *Nelly's Version*, *The Seven Ages* and *Ghosts* published in paperback by Flamingo. She is also the author of *Patriarchal Attitudes*, a seminal work of feminist social criticism.

RELATIVE VALUES

My daughter? She's a writer. Well, not exactly famous, I
wouldn't call her that, but certainly well known. Novels,
she writes novels. I shouldn't think you'd have heard of
her: she's a bit highbrow, what you might call a special-
ised taste. I can't say I'd read her myself if we weren't
related. But you have to make an effort, don't you, when
it's your own flesh and blood? I've got a whole shelf full
of her stuff, and every other year there's a new one and
I know she expects me to say something about it, at least
to prove I've read it. To tell you the truth, sometimes
I'm hard pushed to know what to say, but they expect
you to say something, don't they? It's like when they
were at school. In some ways they never grow up.

What are they like? It's hard to know how to describe
them. Difficult, certainly. I find them hard going, not the
sort of thing I'd go for at the public library. You have to
concentrate really hard, and even then you're sometimes
a bit bewildered. Of course, she'd say reading should be
difficult, and that the reader has to put in an effort too,
if the book is any good. I don't follow this myself, but
then I don't pretend to be a highbrow. I never went to
university or anything like that. Well, girls didn't, in our
day. I was brought up to believe that a woman's first

duty was to keep a happy home, care for her husband and children, and all that sort of thing. But that's considered very old-fashioned now, I know.

Oh yes, she did get married, but it didn't last. Can't say I'm altogether surprised. She's not cut out for domestic life, though God knows I've tried to teach her the basics. But it was very difficult. Whatever you asked her to do, she always had a reason for not doing it. Either she was doing her homework, or she was reading a book, or she was just going out to meet a friend. There was always an excuse, or she'd listen to loud music in her room and pretend not to hear me calling her down to the kitchen. And when she did come down she always had a reason why whatever I'd asked her to do didn't need doing anyhow. If I asked her to dry the dishes she'd say why didn't I let them drain, and that it was unhygienic to use a cloth anyhow. And why couldn't her brother set the table for once, and what was the point of polishing silver if it turned brown in a week, and that it was healthier to eat potatoes with the skin on, so she didn't see the point in peeling them.

She had an answer for everything, even then. Little Miss Clever Dick, I called her. Well, as I said to her, once you've got your own household you can do as you please, but whilst you're living in my house you will do as you're told. She didn't like that, oh no. I had no idea girls could be so wilful. Of course, she'd do it in the end, but there would be one almighty sulk, and she'd do the dishes with a very ill grace. Quite the wrong attitude, in my opinion. After all, these things have to be done, so why not do them cheerfully?

No, she doesn't write under her maiden name. She uses her married name, even though they've been divorced for years. I find it a bit odd, but she says, once you're established, you can't keep chopping and changing. Well, I wouldn't know about these things. But to tell you the truth, I'm quite thankful she doesn't use our name.

First of all, before I begin, I want you to bear one thing in mind. I am a practising writer, and not a professor of literature, so you must not believe a word I say. You laugh, and I am not of course suggesting that you should believe everything your professors tell you, but there is a grain of seriousness in my little joke. My vision is partial, necessarily so, and I often find myself saying things about writing, whether in print or during an interview, which, a moment later, I know to be untrue, or only partially true, even though they were spoken in all sincerity.

Let me give you an example. I could say to you, with my hand on my heart, that my novels are not auto-biographical. Virginia is not me, I never had a sister who committed suicide, my mother is not in the least like Mrs Greenaway, and I do not like cats. Therefore *Open Windows* is in no sense an autobiographical novel. However, it is undoubtedly true that at a deeper level all imaginative writing must have an element of the auto-biographical in it. Where does our knowledge of life come from, if not from our own experience? What are the raw materials from which we weave, except the sights and sounds, the emotions and conflicts and experiences which have surrounded us since birth?

Imagination, I hear you say. Writers are supposed to use their imagination, the gift that separates them from other mortals. But what do we really mean by imagin-ation? Do we mean the capacity to transport the reader to exotic locations and invent endless unlikely adventures that have little or nothing to do with real life as we have experienced it? Of course not. At least, I hope you agree with me that this is not what we look for in good writing. I refer you to Coleridge's distinction between fancy and imagination, which I am sure you know already. To 'imagine' is to have the ability to summon up an image so vividly that the reader lives the moment with you; to think yourself into a given moment, a given situation, so that you are able to recreate it on the page with absolute conviction. Whether that moment ever took place in so-called real life or not is irrelevant. It is just as difficult to write about real events as about imaginary ones when it comes to struggling with words.

So, although *Open Windows* is not an autobiographical novel, in another sense elements of my own experience are bound to be embedded in it. Virginia is not me, nor is Anna. Self-confession is a flood, a sprawling mess, which leads only to an amorphous confusion. Every experienced novelist knows this, and learns to bottle things up in convenient characters. So perhaps it is fair to say that both Virginia and Anna contain fragments of me, insofar as such a statement has any meaning. Likewise, Mrs Greenaway is not my mother. They have little or nothing in common, certainly as far as class, interests, physical attributes, personal history, speech patterns – all the things we associate with the idea of a character in fiction – are concerned. On the other hand, I cannot deny that all my feelings about the nature of the mother-daughter relationship at a given point in history spring from my relationship with my own mother. How could it be otherwise? I am a human being, not a computer, and even computers only throw out what you have fed into them.

Why I'm glad she doesn't use our name? Well, she's not above being a bit spiteful, you know. At least, I call it spiteful. Maybe she's just being thoughtless. That wouldn't be anything new, I'm afraid. She says things in her books which can be really hurtful, and it upsets me. For instance, she wrote this book about a woman with two daughters, and one of them commits suicide. I knew she was getting at me, and it really bothered me. I lay awake half the night, worrying about it. No, I know neither of my children ever took an overdose or anything, and besides, my other child's a boy, but there were lots of little details in it that I recognised. Nobody else would, maybe, but I did, and she must have known I would, and I can't help feeling she did it to get at me. Why else would she do a thing like that?

I don't know that I can give you an example, offhand. It's a while since I read it, and I've tried to put it out of my mind. Oh yes, there's this scene where the mother makes the daughter, the younger one, the one who ends up killing herself, she makes her eat something she's got an aversion to, fried egg, I think it was. This girl is more or less starving herself, what they'd call anorexic these days, I suppose; anyway, she can't stand fried food, and the mother makes her eat this fried egg and the girl is sick afterwards. Well, I know and she knows that I once made her sit up half the night because she wouldn't finish her supper. I expect she's told all her posh friends about it, and maybe even mentioned it in one of those interviews she gives to the newspapers, so no doubt half the world knows about it by now. That's why I'm only thankful she writes under her married name. What would people think? And she wasn't even sick, for the simple reason that she never ate the fish. I remember now, it was haddock. She sat there till nearly midnight, it must have been, her back stiff as a poker, staring at the wall opposite with her mouth tight shut, and wouldn't budge, or eat, or anything. In the end her father made me take the fish away and send her to bed. He always did have a soft spot for her. In his eyes she could do no wrong, to tell you the truth. As a matter of fact we had a row about it afterwards. He said I should have cooked her something else, since I knew she couldn't abide fish. But, as I said to him, you're not the one who does the cooking. You can rack your brains, sometimes, trying to think what to give them. Besides, children should be taught to eat everything that's put in front of them, it's for their own good in the long run.

So fiction writers are essentially liars, but we lie in order to tell the truth, the truth as we see it. We rearrange the truth, if you like, in order to bring out its real meaning. Experience is in itself chaotic, but we all have ways of interpreting what happens to us in order to make sense of our lives, justify what we have done and intend to do in the future, give some kind of meaningful pattern to the things that have happened to us. Up to a point we all do this, and do it quite unconsciously, but the novelist takes the process one stage further, and does it knowingly, and artfully too. Sometimes it is very obvious to the reader: too much has been left out, everything is very schematic, not to say simplistic. Other writers are much more subtle, and do it by a little rearrangement here, a touch of highlighting there, a deepening of certain shadows to bring out the shape of things. Yes, we say, this is just how life is, and we are right to say so, in spite of the deception. For it is only by this subtle and artful rearrangement, this shadowing and highlighting, that we are able to see at all, and make sense of what we see.

Take Mrs Greenaway, for instance, and her relationship with her two daughters in *Open Windows*. One of my purposes in that book was to show how, in a patriarchal system, mothers, who are themselves victims of it, in turn become the active oppressors of their own daughters, not just because they see no way out of the trap in which they themselves are caught, but because they have to justify their own, often petty and futile lives, in order to keep their own sense of self-respect. Now, to bring out the nature of this tragic cycle I made use of a narrative which is, by the standards of everyday life as most of us have experienced it, a bit melodramatic, a bit over the top, as you might say. This was my way of highlighting what I believe to be the essentially destructive and damaging nature of the mother-daughter relationship within a patriarchal society. I could have done it in other ways, but they might have been much more long-winded and you, the reader, would probably have lost interest and stopped reading.

Yes, that's a photo of her on the mantelpiece. She must have been about eight then. I think they're lovely at that age, before they start getting all gawky. She took after her father, not me. Perhaps that's why they were so close, but men always do make a pet of their daughters, don't they? And he was proud of her, because she got good marks at school, but cleverness isn't everything, is it? It made her very hard. But as far as he was concerned, she could do no wrong. More than once I've said to him, it's all very well for you to say let the girl alone, but you're not here half the time. You don't hear the way she talks to me when she's in one of her moods. I mean, children shouldn't answer back like that, should they? I was taught to have respect for my elders, and besides, I've only got one pair of hands, and if a girl can't help a bit in the house, I don't know what the world's coming to. It's all training, isn't it? As I said to her, time and again, you're going to be doing housework for the rest of your life, unless you're lucky enough to marry a very rich man, so you might as well get used to it. But she wouldn't have it, she'd rather have her nose in a book than learn something useful.

That's my son, here, playing with a ball on the back lawn. He's two years younger than her. Yes, he's married, and they've got two children. Oh no, he's not in the literary line, oh dear me no. He's more interested in machinery, mechanically minded, that sort of thing. A proper boy, always was. At the age of ten he could tell you every make of car on the road. I used to show him off to my friends, and none of them ever caught him out. He used to collect those little cars in matchboxes, all his pocket money went on them, and I always had to put one in his stocking at Christmas.

I do not want you to think that this is the only way of interpreting *Open Windows* or even the most important one. Literary texts are open to multiple interpretations, and one reading does not invalidate others. Nor is the author necessarily the best person to interpret a text. I have often found myself thinking that a book I was working on was 'about' a particular theme or topic and discovered, after completing it, that it was really about something else, at a deeper level, of which I was not aware at the time of writing. But I must emphasise that this does not mean that my original intention has been cancelled out.

You are welcome to deconstruct to your heart's content. If you prefer a Freudian reading of the novel, or to see in it Jungian archetypes, that is your choice. But put the text first, do not maul it about and ignore large chunks of it in order to make it fit in with your pet theory. Intelligent reading requires sensitivity and an open mind, an ear for nuances and the capacity to make connections which are not overtly stated. But it also requires common sense. Sometimes a sentence really does mean what it says, and can be taken at face value. Listen to what the author says, as you are listening now, because the author's comments are likely to be nearer the truth than anything a literary critic may have to say. But do not make the mistake of thinking it is the whole truth. It never is.

Yes, I think he takes after me, really. And my father, he's a lot like him. He's got his colouring, whereas I'm a bit darker. His job? Well, he's had a bit of bad luck lately, some difficulty at the firm where he worked, I don't really understand the ins-and-outs of it, but they had to let him go. It's all so different these days, isn't it? No security, not like when we were young, and who could have fore-seen that the car industry wouldn't have been safe for life? He's been in and out of work a number of times, to tell the truth. The last job involved selling, but he was trained to do research and development. Personally, I would have liked him to be a doctor, but it was always cars and motors for him, right from the start. And to be frank, he was never really the studious type, more the outdoor sort. He likes games, football, anything sporty.

Well, he's very practical, down-to-earth. Nothing airy-fairy about him. Both feet on the ground and no nonsense. As I said to her, it's all very well your wanting to be a writer, but where's the money coming from? I mean, most writers, even when they do manage to get things published, don't have two pennies to rub together. You mustn't believe everything you read in the papers, about these million dollar deals, and film rights and the like. We had her learn shorthand and typing, even her father insisted on that. A girl can always make a living with shorthand and typing, and if the worst comes to the worst and she doesn't get married, there's something to fall back on.

In the event she's done rather well, really, I must admit. Got her own flat, and a house in the country, and both her children have been to college. They're quite brainy, take after her, I suppose. And she's always off somewhere, the United States, Sweden, Australia, you name it, she's been there. They pay her fare and everything, you know, all she has to do is make a few public appearances, go on television, that sort of thing. Oh yes, she's on television quite often. I don't really understand it, as I say, her books can be quite depressing. Still, things seem to have worked out for her, and I'm glad we gave her a chance. Girls should be given a chance, same as boys, I always think, if that's what they want. I can't say it hasn't been hard, and we've had to make sacrifices along the way, but nobody can say we didn't give her a chance.

A Double Date

REBECCA BROWN

Rebecca Brown is the author of two novels, *The Haunted House* and *The Children's Crusade* (both in Picador). Her work has also appeared in the anthologies *Mae West Is Dead* (Faber) and *Passion Fruit* (Pandora). She lives in Seattle and London.

A DOUBLE DATE

My mother and I are on a double date. That's what she calls it, but she's being optimistic.

'But we will be on a double date,' she says, 'as soon as we get some guys.'

And that's what she's doing right now, right here at the Empress Court Disco Roller Rink in Southend – trying to get some guys. We're sitting at a sticky-topped, white metal table. Mom is drinking a diet Coke and not eating (she's on her diet again). I'm picking at the mushy spaghetti that's supposed to be the dinner out I'd get if I consented to accompany my mother on her rounds. I'd made a face when the gooey white stuff was slopped onto my plate. The Jewish guy behind the counter had snapped, 'You come here for the Monday Night $1.50 Pasta and Soft Drink Special and you expect the Savoy Grill?' I started to talk back to him, but Mom, who didn't want to waste valuable guy-getting time standing in line, wouldn't let me protest. Mom never protests about things that could get results, like a word to the manager about the crappy food produced by his busted pasta machine. But she's a great one for dancing around about things she can't change – things that no-one can change, things that are done.

Mom and I have pushed the wax paper cup and styrafoam plate of picked-at spaghetti over to the far side of the table. She's retouching her nails, looking at her hair in her compact mirror, scanning the floor for guys, and is still able to keep an eye on me. I'm slumped over my language textbook trying to get some homework done. My English teacher, Mrs Greenaway, always gives lots of homework. Most of the kids hate it, but I don't mind. Homework usually gives me an excuse to hang out at home by myself – i.e. without Mom. Though sometimes, like tonight, she snares me.

'Oh shut that awful book,' says Mom. 'How are you gonna get a guy if your nose is in a book?'

I stare down at the crack between the pages of *Story and Structure* as if I could will one of the characters, like Cyril Biggs, insurance claims investigator, to come to life and drag me outta this hell-hole of a double date with Mom. I press my hands over my ears but I still hear her.

'. . . and how am I gonna get a guy if I'm stuck with a drip like you?'

'Did I ask to come here tonight?' I snap at her.

My mother glares at me over her compact then stabs more lipstick on her mouth.

I slap my hands down on the table. 'Did I ask to be born?'

My mother drops her compact. Her mouth seems to open by itself but no words come out. She blinks then closes her mouth. I start to feel triumphant. This is the only time I've ever been able to shut her up. But it doesn't last for long.

She clears her throat, pats her upper chest like she was coughing, picks up her compact and carries on as if she hasn't heard me. 'Sit up straight. You're slouching again.

You keep on like that and you'll be a humpback by the time you're eighteen. No-one likes a humpback.'

'Aw, Mom,' I sigh, shifting around in my seat.

'And put a smile on your face, for God's sake. Is that so hard?' Mom stretches her lips and parts her yellow teeth in a really plastic smile. 'Try to look pleasant. No-one likes a pouter.'

I bare my teeth.

She turns away from me and looks out at the roller-skaters falling around on the floor. She starts snapping her fingers and nodding her head to the awful disco rhythm that pounds through the cavernous, sweat-sock smelling room.

'Oh look, there's a couple of cute ones!' She points to two boys crashing around on the floor. I grab her hand.

'You don't have to be so obvious,' I hiss. 'You're eyeing them, remember?'

'Eyeing guys' is what she's dubbed this preliminary step to 'getting some guys'. She shoves her compact back into her purse, pats her hair and arranges herself casually in her chair. She looks ridiculous. Her makeup is as bright and sloppy as a little girl playing fancy dress. Her finger-nails and toenails are bright red. Why she's wearing high-heeled, open-toed pumps in a roller rink is beyond me. She shakes her head a little, brushes the sides of her hair back just enough to give herself that windswept look, but not enough to show the grey roots underneath the dye.

'Shit!' she whispers frantically. 'Did I just smear my mascara?'

'No Mom, you're all in place.' Her powder is so thick you could put your finger through it and leave a hole. It looks like Clearasil.

'So whadya think?' She nods at the two boys, she's spotted on the floor. They're fairly indistinguishable from

51

the rest of the gangly, pimply, greasy-haired, peach-fuzzed boys in the room.

'Oh, I don't know. . . .'

But Mom's not listening to me. She's trying to decide which one she likes more, the one with the sweat stains on the armpits of his purple football jersey, or the one with the black socks that show where his jeans are two inches too short. They're both awkward on their skates, all crooked elbows and knees.

She looks down at her clothes to see who she'll match better. This is a big consideration for her. 'A handsome couple should look like a handsome couple,' she always says. Mom is wearing shiny purple leggings and a sleeveless, lavender polyester blouse which is unbuttoned practically down to her navel. Her clothes are tight, shamelessly showing off her bulges and the lines of her underclothes. She has about twenty white and lavender and purple plastic bracelets on her arms and huge fake-rock rings on her fingers. She makes a lot of racket when she tries to discreetly lift the breath spray from her purse and give her mouth a shot. This is the sign that she's going in for the kill.

'Want some?' she whispers conspiratorially, not taking her eyes off the boys. She's on auto-pilot when she asks me this. She isn't aware whether I answer or not. She puts the spray back in her big, white, shiny, fake-leather purse and, without looking at me, orders: 'Get rid of the damn book.'

I close the covers of *Story and Structure* reluctantly. Will Mrs Greenaway believe my excuse when I tell her that my mother wouldn't let me do my homework?

The song is coming to a close and the roller rink DJ is announcing in his best AM voice that he's going to make it a little mellow with a slow song. As the synthesiser strings start up and the boy-girl couples on the floor move close to one another, the boys my mother has been eyeing skate towards the exit nearest the concession stand. Which is of course the exit nearest our table. My mother plans in advance for some things.

'Excuse me, gentlemen,' she wiggles her fingers in the air. The boys bump into each other when they stop to see if someone's talking to them. ''R ya'll goin' t' th' r'freshment booth?' my mother asks in her Southern belle voice.

'Huh?' they ask, taking a step towards us.

'I say-ud, 'r ya'll goin' t' th' r'freshment a-rea?' she asks again, batting her thick blue eyelashes.

'Sure are, lady,' the one with the sweat-stained shirt answers. I hope that the way he says 'lady' will make my mom a little less enthusiastic about her prospects, or at least make her act her age. It doesn't.

'Well, we two girls 'r all alone, 'n there's such a large crowd ova' there.' The boys and I look at the refreshment stand; a couple of ten-year-olds are making slurpy noises in the bottom of their Coke cups; no-one else is in line. 'And we weren't sure if we could get ourselves a lil' small, but oh so r'freshin', cool, iced drink.' She looks down her nose at the cup and plate of spaghetti at the end of the table as if they had been left there by some terribly crude and common person before us.

'Look lady, it's easy. You just go up there –' He points to the stand with his black grimy fingernail.

'You two gentlemen would be so good at t' get us two tired thirsty girls a nice cool drink, wouldn't you?' She produces a frilly hanky and waves it in front of her face as if she finds the plantation heat oppressive.

The two boys look at one another and don't know whether they should respond like their instincts tell them to, and treat my mother like a fresh, pushy girl, or if they should use the manners they've been taught to use when dealing with the weird adult acquaintances of their parents.

'Uh sure,' the one with the black socks answers, 'uh . . . whadyou and your –'

'Sister!' my mother interjects triumphantly. 'We're sisters, aren't we?' She flashes me a toothy smile while she squeezes my leg beneath the table. I flinch. I wish my mother would die of a brain tumour.

'I'm the older sister,' she laughs, 'though only slightly older. My name is – Shana.' (My mother's name is Louise). 'And this is my sister,' she pauses, 'Ruth. She's the shy one.'

Beneath the table she gouges my kneecap. 'I'm sure these two gentlemen won't bite if y' offer them a smile, Ruth,' my mother says. I glare at the plate of spaghetti. If I could feed her into the funnel of a pasta machine and grind her out in strands of spaghetti or linguini or rotini or fusili or just plain fatty beef, I would.

'Uh . . .' the one with socks says, sticking out his hand, 'I'm Stephen.' My mother releases my leg from her fingers and lifts her hand for the boy to kiss. He reaches his hand further to her, but when she doesn't take it to shake, he shrugs and drops it.

'So whadya want?'

'Oh, we'll trust you men,' she lowers her voice when she calls them this to sound hoarse and suggestive, 't' get us somethin' y' think we'd like.'

They hesitate a moment waiting for us to get our money for our drinks. The purple shirt boy sneezes and wipes his nose with his forearm. I start to reach into my pocket and get some change when my mother stops me.

'I'm sure these gentlemen would be ver' happy t' buy

some drinks f' two most grateful girls. It might even help their chances of winnin' a turn on the' dance flo' with us!'

'Oh, God,' I clap my hands over my eyes so they can't see how embarrassed I am. Why couldn't my mother have been killed in a train crash in Holland?

For some reason the boys don't make a protest or even snicker at the fool my mother is, but obediently trot off to the refreshment booth.

'We'll save yo' seats!' my mother shouts after them with a wave of her hanky. As if the two ratty chairs at the far end of the table were box seats to the Royal Birthday Gala at the Paris Ballet. She clutches the back of the empty chair beside her desperately.

When they're out of hearing distance my mother balls the hanky up in her fist, leans over to me and hisses, 'Never offer to pay for your drinks. You mustn't let them think you can do anything. They need to feel in control.'

'But Mom, I don't want to be friends with anybody you need to be like that with –'

'Don't be an asshole, you little shit, we're not talking about friends, we're talking about men.'

'Oh, Jesus,' I sigh.

'And don't let them hear you swear. They don't like girls who talk like whores.'

'Oh, come on, Mom, don't tell me –'

'I'll tell you something, Miss Back-Talk, you disagree with them the way you're disagreeing with me right now and they'll walk straight out that door.' She points dramatically to the red EXIT light. 'And do you know what happens when they walk out that door, Miss Smart-Ass? I'll tell you what happens. Your meal ticket walks out that door. And you're left sitting in some lousy goddamn dump, like where you and your godforsaken mother live, without a dime in your goddamn lousy pocket and all you have to your goddamn name is some squawking goddamn back-talking brat telling you what to do. Is that what you want?'

I'm glad the song on now is 'Good Time Night', a really loud, fast marathon of a song, because I don't want anyone to hear what she says to me. I wish I couldn't hear her.

'Is that what you want?' my mother asks again, leaning over the table toward me.

I look at my mother, but I don't say anything. I try to blur my eyes so I don't see the worry line on her forehead, the sharp wrinkles that break down from her frown. I try to see what's past her. I try to visualise the counter of the refreshment booth, the red plastic bottle of ketchup and the yellow one of mustard and the glass and aluminium shaker of Parmesan cheese.

'Do you hear me young lady?'

But I can't see past my mother's face.

'Yes,' I say quietly.

'Then put a goddamn smile on your face and get to work.'

I try to smile a real-looking one for her, but I don't know how, yet, to make myself look how I need to look. She wipes her forehead with her hanky, then opens her purse again. I turn away from her and try to look at the people skating around on the roller rink floor in front of us. A little kid clings to her Mom, then falls and whines. A gang of kids my age, the age my mother wishes she could be again, before her life became like it is now, are hanging onto each other trying to cop a feel or steal a kiss or grab a fistful of ass. I look away from them, ashamed to be my age. I spot a grey-haired couple holding hands and skating smoothly around the edge of the ring. They swing so sweetly with one another. When he lifts her up, like Fred Astaire, her wide skirt ripples in a perfect arc. I wonder how they can be so graceful with each other when everyone else around them is so seedy. Oblivious to the brash disco rhythm, they sway with one another to a tune no-one else hears.

Mom is staring at the skate floor, her face stiff with her plastic smile. The muscles on her jaws are tense. Her eyes are glazed. I wonder what she's looking for beyond the scene in front of her.

As this song is ending, the grey-haired woman puts her hand on her partner's arm. Their heads lean towards each other and their shoulders shake with very private laughter. They lead one another to an exit on the other side.

'They're on their way,' Mom whispers. She nods towards the boys who are paying at the concession stand. Mom has a quick final check of her lipstick and eyeliner, sprays her mouthspray again, and pulls her hair back in a neat, tight bun. That's odd – she usually goes for the windswept look. I look away from her desperate attempt to be attractive.

When one of the boys places my drink on the table for me, I start to say, 'Oh, thank you so much!' the way Mom's taught me to, but I'm speechless. When I look up, I see Mom's lost the wrinkles near her mouth and the worry line on her forehead. She looks like she's shed twenty pounds and about as many years. She doesn't bulge out of her polyester blouse, but is trim and firm in her dancer's full-length leotard.

'Sh-Shana?' I try to ask, but she doesn't answer.

The boy who's putting mother's drink in front of her has changed as well. Instead of the oily peach fuzz on his cheek, he's got a firm, clean-shaven jaw and his skin is clear. Instead of wearing a sweaty football shirt, his chest is bare. The muscles on his upper arms are neat and taut

as limes. I see his thighs flex under his leotard as he bends
over my mother. She takes a single sip from her thin-
stemmed glass of water then puts the glass back on the
ratty table. Her boy is offering her his hand. She takes it
and they step out to the dance floor.

Stunned, I watch the chorus of dancers part for them.
I turn to ask the boy who's brought my Coke to me
what's happened, but he's changed too. The hand that he
holds out to me is confident and strong. I take his hand
self-consciously. I'm the only one who hasn't changed.
My roller skates clomp on the hardwood floor as I tag
along behind my handsome partner. I can barely stand up
in the heavy skates, much less dance in them, but I try to
act like I'm supposed to. I hang onto his torso, embarrassed to feel his warm, firm, slightly sweaty skin. I try
to bounce to the disco song I hear, but he is moving to
a slow and fluid rhythm.

When I feel his hands against my hips, I tingle. I don't
know if I want to skate with him or run away. I clutch
his shoulders but I can't hold him. My hands slide off his
shoulders as he spins me by my hips. My skates whirl. I
can't control my feet. Everything moves so fast it blurs.
I close my eyes but I just feel dizzy. I reach my hands out
to grab him because I want to stop. 'Stop,' I say. 'Please
stop.' I don't know if he hears me – I can hardly hear
anything except the sound of my body spinning – but
he releases me. He slips his fingers from my skin and,
unattached, I spin. My arms flail trying to grab something. I fall. As I tumble down onto the hard, ungiving
ground, I see him lift his perfect naked arms above his
head. The tips of his pretty, slender fingers touch. His
stomach and chest are smooth, his thighs are tight. He
kicks up his feet and leaps away as sudden as a sprite. I
try to see where he lands but I don't think he ever comes

down. I don't hear the thud of his feet on the ground. What I hear is a sound like radio static, the way it sounds when you drive long distance with the stations fading in and out. The disco beat is drowned by the swell of an orchestra.

I lie on the floor, my body aching, while the rest of the chorus of dancers swings upstage then disappears. The only couple centre stage is my mother and her partner who perform a *pas de deux*. When he puts his hands upon her hips, I feel them on my own. He starts to spin her. I want to warn her. I start to shout but my child's voice cannot be heard above the orchestra. I try to stand on my skates and go to her but, baby-like, I fall. He spins my mother close to me. He spins her faster and faster. Every time he spins her, she is younger and more beautiful. Her eyes are closed. Her eyelids tremble. Her neck and her smooth white chest above her leotard shine with sweat. Her hands are clenched, her mouth is slightly open.

When I look at the blurry rapture on my mother's spinning face, I see, as clearly as if it has already happened, what will happen: that he will take his hands from her, that she will spin, that she will fall with me. But I don't want to stop them. For, like her I am dizzy, open-mouthed and speechless with the brief and solitary joy which she finds in my father's hands, the night their bodies ask me to be born.

The Dinosaurs of Love

KATE PULLINGER

Kate Pullinger was born in British Columbia, Canada, in 1961. In 1982 she left Canada and came to London where her short stories began to appear regularly in magazines such as *New Statesman, Fiction* and *Spare Rib*. In 1986 she won the *City Limits* short story competition and in September 1987 took up the post of Writer in Residence at Battersea Arts Centre. Her first collection of short stories, *Tiny Lies*, was published by Jonathan Cape in 1988, and her first novel, *When the Monster Dies*, in 1989.

THE DINOSAURS OF LOVE

In late October the sleet drives cold and hard in Toronto and at night the dark streets are slick and shiny with black ice. A carelessly-placed foot will slide out suddenly, as if about to take flight, as though the foot has become a football. The rest of the body crumples and falls, thud, onto the hard sidewalk. Scraped, bruised, damp and cold, a moment spent lying on the pavement seems an eternity.

Magda dreamt she was lying on icy ground when in fact she was lying in the arms of the Saint, her current neo-punk boyfriend. Saint was long and bony and hard, his skin cool and a bit bumpy; Magda woke up on top of him, chilled. She rolled over and wrapped herself in their cast-off duvet, rubbing her arms to get warm. She felt like a dinosaur, slow-witted and unwieldy. Saint slept on, unaware, and Magda dozed off again.

When she next woke up it was morning and Saint was already in the kitchen making coffee. He carried two mugs into the bedroom and got back into bed. Magda watched him lazily, eyeing his body which, although cold, she found exciting. 'I think,' murmured Saint, 'we should dress in matching clothing and wear our hearts on our sleeves. We'll start a new fashion.'

'In Toronto,' answered Magda, 'if you wore your heart

on your sleeve it would freeze. Even a heart the size of a man would begin to beat sluggishly, the blood become slushy, the tempo out of time. And matching clothes – we'd look like American tourists.'

'You are an American,' said Saint in his self-righteous Canadian way, as if simply being an American automatically conferred upon Magda some sort of moral depravity. Magda sipped her coffee and let his barb slide by; it found nothing to snag on her smooth skin. Saint ran his hand over her breast. His fingers felt freeze-dried; she shuddered.

After Magda lost at Wimbledon she gave up tennis, California, her cosmetic-surgery-addict of a mother, a Porsche, her tennis coach husband, five million dollars worth of product endorsement contracts, her pasta machine and her monthly hair peroxide treatments. Early one morning, before even the cleaning ladies were awake, she took a cab to the empty airport, and, rubbing sleep into her eyes, bought a ticket to somewhere she had never been. Canada meant very little to her then, somewhere North, big and far away. It was not that she had felt humiliated at Wimbledon or that she had in any way been disgraced; it was more that she had suddenly felt totally and obnoxiously bored. Perhaps it had been something that Veronica, her dancer friend in London, had said that triggered her decision. That story about the girl with a faked brain tumour – it had all seemed so inexplicable at the time – made Magda feel tired and drained. In the face of such gargantuan self-deception, everything else seemed silly and futile. And Veronica herself had seemed so cynical and worn out; they had gone to the cinema and argued about the facts of life. Still, after that, the thought of hitting yet another tennis ball back and forth over a net made her own brain ache. Magda had never really liked professional tennis; that, along with the blonde hair, had been her mother's idea. 'That is it,' she said to herself on the plane home, 'I'm gone.'

In Toronto she told no-one about her previous career and, dressed in black with her dark hair growing in, no-one recognised her. After daily workouts at the YMCA she applied her careful but relatively thick make-up (she still felt a need for disguise) and went out on the cold, windy streets. Toronto was not like California. Even the city's plans to cover over one of the small islands in Lake Ontario and create a mini-Florida did not make it more like California. The stock exchange that mimicked Wall Street and the fact that everyone knew who Mickey Mouse was did not make Canada American and Magda felt pleased by this. The bizarre Canadian-ness of Saint made her happy as well; she almost felt she belonged once they moved in together – at least she belonged to him.

In eastern Canada the autumn is marked by the fall of the leaves from the trees. Green becomes red, yellow and orange, gold stands out starkly against the black bark of the beeches, colours that neither words, paints, nor dyes can possibly recreate. Magda had not expected this marvel and felt overwhelmed; she looked at Saint with new respect. 'You live though this agony of beauty and regeneration every year,' she thought as she lay next to his cold, hard body. While the cups of coffee iced over she and Saint made love and, afterwards, he had fallen back asleep. 'Every year the leaves fall orange and red, splattered with blood and Hallowe'en, and still your life as Saint continues without pausing, and the lives of other Saints like you simply go on.'

As the trees slowly changed, Magda was changing too. She moved through the streets of the hard, uptight city less aggressively than she had initially, she became more willing to fall behind. She often walked along **Bloor Street** and, crossing the Humber River, would stare from the high bridge down at the water as it snaked its way through the colours. She rode the subway with reluctance preferring the more stately and scenic progression of the street-cars. The air was laden with autumnal longing; the whole city seemed to be waiting. Magda wondered if people were simply cooling down after the hot summer, stalling and lingering until the first snowfall came and laid its winter weight on their shoulders.

Still able to afford not to work – if anything, her career had been lucrative – Magda spent hours sitting in Polish cafés reading novels. On the days Saint had off from the restaurant – he was a chef – they visited art galleries and exhibitions. They went to the Royal Ontario Museum and spent a long time lingering over the dinosaurs. With their woollen hats, gloves and scarves temporarily stored in the cloakroom, Saint seemed expansive and kept swearing softly and exclaiming, 'I wonder how they had sex?' Magda, however, could think only of the Ice Age which she knew approached these mammoths at play; she thought it all must have seemed quite inexplicable at the time.

At night Magda and Saint slept with the bedroom window open. Saint claimed the room was too hot and he needed the fresh air in order to maintain his low body temperature. Being cold-blooded meant he never needed to buy a winter coat. Magda curled up and willed her pulse to slow down. The wind blew outside and sometimes leaves were swept in past the billowing curtains. Purple, gold, and brown, they stuck to the wall opposite like prints made by children. Seeing this, Magda felt like a little girl, thrilled by discovery. In the blue morning light she nudged Saint and said, 'Wake up.'

Saint moaned. He was dreaming. Magda kissed him and shook his head with her hands. He opened his eyes and said, 'When I woke up, the dinosaur was still there.'

'What?' asked Magda.

'Nothing,' replied Saint, shaking his head himself. 'I was dreaming, that's all.'

Song of the Jewish Princess

MICHELENE WANDOR

Michelene Wandor is a poet, playwright and critic as well as a writer of prose fiction. Her most recent publications include *Guests in the Body*, a collection of short stories published by Virago in 1986, and *Look Back in Gender*, on the family and sexuality in drama, published by Methuen in 1987. Her dramatisations include *The Wandering Jew* (National Theatre) and *The Brothers Karamazov* (Radio 4). Her *Selected Poems* will be published in 1990, and she is currently working on a novel set in the sixteenth century.

SONG OF THE JEWISH PRINCESS

My thunderer blew in through the door, autumn leaves swirling behind him, green and brown scraps of the fading year barbed on the frayed strands of his wild woollen cloak, dry twigs pinned on his shoulders under the wide strap that held his bag, one lone leaf poised like a dancer on the brim of his hat.

Today, he who was always on time, he who always closed doors behind him, he who held himself carefully in his own space, today he was tousled, windswept, his cheeks red, his nose glowing and bulbous, his eyes wrinkled against the winter wind, his mouth taut with hurry and cold against the grin that I knew could warm his face. Well, he said, what are you waiting for?

I hushed my body's desire to rush to him, and began to play.

I am the original Jewish princess. The authentic article. The instrument on which the real music, according to the text, can be played. Play me. I shall sound true to you.

It was a long day, stopping only for wine and bread, and the bitter goats' cheese Carlos had brought with him. He worked himself and us hard and did not talk to me, except to make points about the music. By early evening, I was shivering with tiredness and expectation. As we all walked through the cold stone halls to the Hall of Mirrors, I huddled into my own deep blue woollen cloak, the colour of the evening summer sky. Coming in from the cold, the wave of heat in the Hall hit me full in the face. The guests hardly noticed our arrival, and scarcely nodded an ear in our direction as we began to play. As usual, Ferdinand and Isabella talked throughout, though I knew that any flaw in the performance would invoke sarcasm the following day.

Halfway through the evening, some late guests arrived, and as the huge wooden doors were opened to admit them, the gusting wind blew out all the candles – except for two; one behind me and one behind Carlos. Momentarily the Hall was in silence, and without any sense of pre-planning, Carlos and I began playing our star piece of the evening; strings, wind and voices flashed into the dark, and between verses Carlos and I improvised. For the first time that day he and I looked full at each other, our eyes, so alike, green flecked with brown, flashing across the Hall, each lured by the pool of light behind the other's head. I swear that we invented fire that night. Flame spiralled and pirouetted between our notes, and for those few moments, the chatterers were silenced.

At the end, the ripples of music bowed their way into the corners of the Hall, and we were applauded. Carlos nodded his head at me, in approval and desire.

I can pick up any instrument and bow or pluck or blow and it will speak. My mother was the same. The bow cuts deep and springy into the string and I curve my body in reply.

When Carlos came into my room, he shut the door quietly and carefully. We still did not speak. Under my blue woollen cloak, his body felt as familiar to me as my own. His green eyes held mine and as we deepened into each other, our movements fitted easily, as they always had.

Play me. I shall sound true to you.

Later we lay, my face nuzzled into Carlos's armpit, smelling cloves and camomile mixed with the acrid savour of satisfaction. There is something I must tell you, he said. I caught my breath. You're going back to her, I said, I knew it. It was only a matter of time.

He flipped himself over on top of me so that he could look at me. It isn't that, Isabella, he said. I began to cry. Every time I see you, I said, I feel it's for the last time. She won't let go. You can't leave the children. I hate goats' cheese.

He put his hand over my mouth. I bit his fingers. Isabella, he said, you must listen. And then he whispered. He was late this morning because he had heard that before very long all infidels would be banished from Spain. I am Jewish, Isabella, he said softly, and you know what that means. I must leave before I am killed.

I stroked him. I knew you were Jewish, I said. Not just because of this – many men are circumcised in this world of mixed races. I just knew. You couldn't know, he said. Not in the way the Inquisition will know, not in the way – I interrupted: I'm coming with you, I said. No – he began. This time I put my hand over his mouth. Then I told him about my mother.

Never have an affair with a musician, she said. A scribe, a soldier, a goat farmer if you must, but not a musician. When I was tiny, she let me pluck the strings on her fiddle, showed me how she tightened the tension, let me hold the bow in my fat hand and promised that one day I would be able to play as she did.

She was right about that, although she did not live to hear it. She also didn't live to see me disregard her advice about musicians. No doubt she would have smiled. My father, you see, was an itinerant musician, a man from North Africa, a Jew, a wandering minstrel who probably left behind him as many children as musical memories. He came to our village one night, in the height of summer. My mother's husband was away in the mountains, with the goats. It was late, no-one saw him arrive. My mother gave him shelter. He played to her. The next morning he wrapped his Ud, the instrument which is so like the courtly lute that every amateur plays here, and he disappeared. My mother described his fingers like spider's webs, trailing and caressing the strings, no frets to hurdle the fingers, allowing him to bend their tunes to his will. He was dark skinned. With green eyes.

My mother told me all this the night before she died. The soldiers came, looking for infidels. My mother was Jewish, but she thought no-one knew. She told me the story about my father, gave me her blue woollen cloak, and made me go and hide with the goats. Her charred body was flung on the ground some days later. I think about her often. I wonder how long it took for the thick earth to rot her flesh. I prefer to think about that than to wonder what the Inquisition did to her. I also worry, because I cannot remember the colour of her eyes.

When a string is ready to snap, it plays sharper and sharper. It cries for the attention that can do it no good. My life is fraying at the edges. I begin not to sound true to myself.

The following afternoon, two musicians, carrying instruments, strolled towards the town walls. Carlos and I also each carried a small phial of poison. His alchemist friend assured him that anyone who took it would fall asleep long before the poison began to eat them away. We promised each other through our tears that we would die rather than be subjected to torture.

The soldiers on guard by the town walls laughed and applauded as we cavorted with our fiddles, mad court musicians aping their wandering minstrel brethren, a lower caste, vulgar and uncertain and despicable. So harmless and silly were we, that they allowed us to wander through the gates and serenade a flock of goats herded on a hill opposite.

I have left my texts behind me.

We slept in a field. Next day, lulled by the quiet of the countryside, we were reckless. A small town, sleepy in the early afternoon haze, suddenly came alive with shouts and screams. Soldiers and locals chased a small group of people, men, women and children. An old man tripped and fell, just beyond the entrance to the alley in which we hid. The crowd kicked him bloody and limp. Then they hurtled past us, knocking us aside and when they had passed, Carlos was no longer with me. I waited, huddled in an abandoned house, hoping he would come back. When it was dark I searched a little. The streets were strewn with dead and wounded. No-one dared to touch them. I dared not stay.

I have had to learn how to improvise all over again.

Memory can be kind. I remember endless roads and fields,

green streaked with brown, brown with green. I could not eat. I felt sick all the time. My fiddle opened doors to me, gave me beds and food. I took it all, and more often than not gave it to the next beggar I met on my way. I searched every face for the familiar mouth, for the green eyes. I learned that northern Italy, Mantova, Ferrara, Venezia even, were the places to go. I hardly noticed that my periods seemed to have stopped. The road changed everything. In any case, the real me was somewhere else, with a man whose hair curled over his collar, whose crooked nose could wrinkle in glee, whose eyes were like mine.

When I finally cried, my imagination flooded out of me. I bled for four days as I had never bled before. Now I knew that Carlos and his child were gone from me for ever. To the rest of the world, he had never been. To me, he could never be again; neither cloaked in rage, nor clear in love. Just misty in my music as I played.

My text comes from the heart. Nothing can be more authentic.

Giovanni has brown eyes. He is kind. He is good. He is my rock. He is calm and decisive, and he waits for me to love him. I should love him. I am grateful to him. After all, he picked me out, a grubby, weary, wandering minstrel, travelling round Italy, playing anywhere, and he made me into the highest in the land – in the region, anyway. I am the Duchess. Of course, no-one knows that I am Jewish. Merely that I am Spanish. I speak Italian impeccably, but with a soft, sibilant accent. When I am asked when I left Spain, I say 1490; if I told them the true year, 1492, they might associate it with the expulsion of the Jews and wonder.

Giovanni is much older than I am. His first wife died in childbirth. The son, a wayward child, was sent to fight with Giovanni's mercenary army against the Turk. Make a man of him, they said. When he returns, he will be Giovanni's heir. So it does not matter that I do not seem able to conceive. I can make love when Giovanni desires, except that for me there is no love in it, just gratitude.

I ached so much from wandering. I had to stop. This seemed the only way. Here I continue to play as I please. My musicians are the finest in the region, envied by the whole of northern Italy. I even pay them on time.

When my strings have settled, you can play me. Then I shall sound true to you.

And then, on a rough, blustery winter day, Carlo came home. Here in the north, in the vast flat plain, on the river that flows to the sea, it rains and rains. Nothing is ever free of mud.

The concert was almost over. I played in the last piece. Just as we were about to begin, the door burst open and a young man thundered in, bringing gusting rain and leaves with him, cloak flung over one shoulder, rough boots, a crooked nose, hair curling down over his shoulders.

I played just for him, my heart pounding, my arm quivering, my sound small and sweet. His eyes were on me the whole time, burning me in tune.

Every text contains within it the music of a thousand others.

The next day Carlo came to see me. A young man, weathered, with no sign of the previous night's thunderer.

Teach me to play, he said. Teach me to play like you. He looked at me, and in his eyes I saw Carlos again, and the baby I had never known, and something else, someone new, whose body was as familiar as my own, and whom I could not touch except strictly in the line of duty, to show how to balance the instrument, to show how to hold the bow, how to flex the wrist, how to find the notes.

He was an exemplary pupil. He rewarded my efforts by working hard and throwing himself into the music like a child. He hated being a soldier, he told me. He was not going to be a ruler. He wanted to be a wandering minstrel, to go on the road, to live free of all ties and responsibilities. I teased him. You're too spoiled, I said. And I gave him the most fiendish musical exercise I could conjure up, as if that would keep him with me for longer.

Let us play our texts to each other. Perhaps we shall sound true.

There was nothing I can think of that precipitated the crisis. One day he blundered through everything, careless, discordant, sullen. When he finished I exploded. Why? He flung his bow on the ground. You, he said. I cannot play to you. You create the conditions of performance. Who do you think you are? You make me nervous.

I am your audience, I said. If you can play to me, you can play to anyone. I can't play to you, he said. Then you'll never make it on the road, I taunted. Music happens because of you, not because of the road. But you're such a natural, he said. Who taught you? No-one, I said. I taught myself. I learned as I travelled. I learned as I played in fields and I learned as I played in courts. You're the real thing, he said, the authentic article.

He said it with sadness, his shoulders dropped, his back bowed, his legs apart, his elbows on his knees, his fingers clamped together in a double fist. A lock of hair fell forward over his face. I lifted it and one finger brushed his cheek. He looked up, his eyes green, just like mine.

I am newly strung, with fine gut, translucent, springy. Play me. I dare you.

What can I tell you. That in the moonlight, in the haven of my tower room, the room of my music, his body felt more familiar than my own. That his skin was warm where mine was cool, and mine warm where his was cool. That we fitted easily until we were the same temperature and could not tell who was who, and he was not Carlos, and he was not a baby, and he was not my stepson and I did not know who he was.

You have everything you want, he said, his cheek against my breast. You have a husband who adores you. You are gifted. You are beautiful. Guilty, my young lord, I said. Don't call me young, he said sharply. I am sorry, I said, my hand on his belly, where the pulses fluttered. I stroked him calm. You know nothing about me, I said. I have heard you play, he said. That is enough.

I am not what I seem, I said. I don't care, he said, I should have married you. I cried and he kissed my face. He smelled of cloves and rosemary and permanence.

And then the door was kicked down.

It takes only a split second to snap. Much longer to be tuned.

Tonight I shall take poison. I shall go out into the dark. I shall cross the river by the small stone bridge that curves over the water at an angle. I shall turn right on the opposite bank and walk along by the river for a few paces until I am opposite the tower in which Carlo and I made love.

I am taut.

The guards let me have my fiddle this evening. They think my husband is wrong to have his adulterous wife beheaded. I think he is wrong too; but he knows that he has no alternative at his own court. If he let me live, he would have to face me every day, and see his son in my eyes.

   The guards have brought me my cloak and the cushion on which Carlo and I lay. I shall put the cushion between me and the cold, damp stone. I shall wrap myself in my deep blue cloak. I shall drink the poison. I shall fall asleep before it begins to tear me apart.

I am the real thing. The first Jewish princess. The authentic instrument on which the musical text can be played. Play me. I shall sound true to you.

In sunlight the river is green. My mother's eyes were green.

Summer School

DIANE PEARSON

Diane Pearson was born in Surrey and passed much of her life in a country village. She began writing in her teens, but it was not until 1967 that her first book *The Marigold Field* was published. *Sarah Whitman* followed in 1971 and in 1975 her bestseller *Csardas* appeared, followed in 1984 by *The Summer of the Barshinskeys*. Diane Pearson now lives in South London with her actor husband and two cats, and works as an editor with a London publishing house.

SUMMER SCHOOL

I hasten to say that accepting an invitation to teach creative writing at a writers' summer school is *not* something I would normally consider. I suppose failed writers have to go somewhere for their summer holidays, but I find I really have nothing to say to them. Alas, they usually have something to say to me – far too much – and it is invariably so trite that I find I am reduced to dialogue as banal as theirs. In any case, I dislike talking about writing at all unless it is to my own small circle of friends who appreciate what I am trying to achieve in my work. I detest those kinds of dinner parties where people, who appear to be intelligent, ask questions like, 'And what do you write?' That happened to me last week when I found myself sitting next to a professional actor who obviously thought he was being terribly charming. 'What do you write?' he asked. 'Literature', I said, and turned to the man on my left for the rest of the evening.

But two factors made me think again about teaching at the Writers' School that particular summer. One was to help out my friend who should have been taking the course herself but had to back out at the last moment because of some trouble with her mother. You know my friend – she's the author of *Open Windows*, that fantastic novel that got reviewed so well and even got onto the bestseller list. Well, actually, it isn't *quite* as fantastic as everyone says but I was pleased that she did so well with it, poor dear. She does have the most awful problems with this frightful old mother who is constantly embarrassing her and sending for her at inconvenient times – like this particular occasion when my friend was supposed to be teaching creative writing and she had a telephone call to say the old harridan had fallen over and broken her hip. Thank God I made *quite* sure I never had any problems of that kind with my mother. When she came back from South Africa after marriage number four had failed I made our relationship very plain. We have no relationship, I explained, and never had. You cannot dump a daughter when she is seven years old and expect to have a relationship. I believe she is living in a residential hotel somewhere on the south coast now.

Anyway, that was one reason for accepting the teaching course, to help out my friend. The other was, well, to be frank, money. They were offering rather a good fee, plus a week's board and first class travel both ways. I'd been badly let down by my publisher that year. I'd been expecting a good royalty cheque at the half year accounting and all I got was a statement showing that I hadn't even earned out the advance. Not, I hasten to add, that my dreary publisher pays anything like a decent advance – it was ridiculously low considering the kind of reviews and critical acclaim I get, but even so that last book hadn't earned out and it looked as though it was going to be a rather sticky six months.

The course I'd been offered didn't look too bad either – 'Creative Writing of the Contemporary Experimental Novel'. That gave me a pretty free hand and probably those on the course would be rather more interesting than the usual kind of aspirants who attend writing schools.

I must confess I was a little disappointed on the first day to discover that, of the sixty-odd people attending the school, only five signed on for my classes – but I suppose that is a pretty fair representation of the proportion of those who can really write and those who merely make a living at it. Let's face it, good, clever, intelligent writing has nothing to do with writing books that people buy and read. And that was one of the things I was going to teach on my course.

Of the five, two I dismissed at once as not worth bothering about; one, a drearily clever young man with a double first from Oxbridge who thought he was going to put me in my place with rhetorical argument and a scathing tongue. I coped with him as I always do with people I don't like, by totally ignoring him, treating him as though he wasn't there, and by the second day he left my course and went to irritate someone else. The other non-starter was a retired doctor who just took reams of notes and asked fatuous questions. I'd met his kind before. He was, on the whole, harmless and didn't interfere with the rest of the class. The other three were definitely interesting, different.

When I walked into my study room on the first day a very fat young-to-middle-aged woman stood up and smiled at me.

'Miss Cavendish,' she said, in a light young voice. 'I'm so thrilled to meet you at last. I've read every one of your books and the last one, *Death and Weddings of a Montenegrin Saddle Maker* made me so excited I couldn't sleep for two nights. Thank you for allowing me to attend your course.'

Her name was Louise Mitchell, and it was on that first day I realised she was one of the promising ones.

As the theme of my course I had taken the short story by Augusto Monterroso, 'When I woke up, the dinosaur was still there'. I made them analyse the brilliance of that short story, and then I asked them to write either one, or at the most two, sentences as profound and meaningful as Monterroso's. The fat young woman wrote,

'It was when I was told I was dying of a brain tumour that I decided to apply for a place at the Writers' Summer School.'

Contrived? Yes, a little I suppose. Possibly even ludicrous, but intriguing too. Did she intend it as black humour or a piece of shocking surrealism? We discussed it, in group, at great length and her responses were intelligent and enthusiastic. In fact the discussion became so animated (once I'd got rid of the Oxbridge young man) that we spent the whole day talking about her story and indeed about her. I thought later that perhaps I had been a little ungenerous to the other members of the class in devoting so much attention to her and I resolved to devote myself to the other two the following day.

The next promising pupil was a funny little man called Cyril Biggs. I can't remember now what his story was, but he had flashes that were quite interesting and what was odd was that, while he looked so ordinary, so boringly ordinary, he was actually teeming with resentment and frustration and bitterness at the unfairness of his life. I understood that terribly well – I really did. If he hadn't been a rather dreary little insurance claims inspector I might have suggested keeping in touch with him when the course had ended.

The other interesting pupil was quite a young girl –

young for a writers' school most certainly – and her short story I do remember very well indeed.

'My mother had yellow teeth and dressed like a young girl. She made me go on double dates with her. I was glad when she died.'

And that I could relate to as well – very, very well. I understood about mothers and daughters better than anyone. Mothers are killers.

So there I was with my three really interesting pupils and as the week progressed we worked very well together. I felt I was actually helping people with potential – people who might indeed, one day, become *true* writers. The daytime sessions were the better part of that writing week – the only good part in fact – for the evenings in the lecturers' common room were sheer hell – mostly because of Mavis Ormitage.

All the lecturers were supposed to stay together during the evenings, partly to 'rest' us from our voracious pupils, and also to exchange ideas and conversation with one another. We were different you see. We were all successful writers and so had something in common. What on earth I was supposed to have in common with someone like Mavis Ormitage I cannot begin to imagine.

She made her full, revolting impact on the very first night. She was sitting in the common room, a huge, ponderous creature with coarse black hair and a wheezy chest. She gave me what I can only describe as a barmaid's grin and said, 'Come in, love. You must be Margaret Cavendish because I know everyone else. I come every year – teach the Trues, I do. Have a drink, dear. Help yourself. Excuse me not getting it for you, once I'm down in the chair I stay here. Would you mind getting me another g & t while you're there.'

I couldn't use my usual technique of ignoring her.

There was this pretence of civility in the common room and Mr Bennett who ran the school made a great and awful art of including everyone in conversation. So it was I found myself forced to talk at length to writers who were taking courses ranging from historical romances to radio plays. But none of them were as repellent as Mavis Ormitage who did the Trues.

She was loud. She was greedy. Frequently during the evening she drank too many g & t's and became sozzled and maudlin. She pried, asked impertinent questions about my background, my parents, whether I'd ever been married (I'd wiped that traumatic experience from my mind totally and wasn't prepared to let a great beached whale like Mavis Ormitage stir it up). She even poked her big round nose into my teaching course, wanted to know on what theme I was basing my class and warning me about Louise Mitchell.

'Don't take that one too seriously, Margaret,' she wheezed. 'She's been coming here for five, six years and she tells a few tall tales. Pretends to be great friends with Veronica Spencer – you know, the ballerina. Says she had an operation for a brain tumour once and that the surgeon fell in love with her. Talks a lot of nonsense, poor sad creature.'

That really annoyed me. How *dare* she be patronising about *my* pupils. She couldn't begin to understand the creative impulses of a mind like Louise Mitchell's. On the experimental novel course we all understood that fantasy is reality and words can make anything believable, especially lies.

'She's rather gifted – unusual,' I said coldly.

'Oh yes, she's that all right. She came on my Trues course once. She's quick and bright O.K. But she didn't get all the attention she wanted in my class. Too many people all working too hard to listen to Louise. She'll do better with someone like you.'

She gave me her barmaid smile again and then leaned over and, with a fat sweaty hand, she patted my shoulder.

'You'll be O.K., love,' she said. 'I know it's difficult being the new girl here, but you're doing a great job, everyone says so. And it's just as important to teach a small class as a big class like mine. After all, dear, you do real writing, don't you, not a lot of rubbish like me.'

'Thank you,' I moved away so as to remove her hand from my shoulder.

'Tell you the truth,' she said. 'I always wanted to write something a bit more ambitious myself. Never wanted to be Queen of the Trues, but never had much choice.'

'We all have a choice,' I replied. 'We make our own lives. Where we are and what we do is entirely up to us. We choose our own direction and we have no-one but ourselves to blame if we find we're doing something we don't like.'

I had actually succeeded in crushing the woman! That huge swarthy face sank into dewlaps and she was momentarily still. I suddenly realised she was a lot older than I'd thought – not fifty but nearer sixty. Fat people often look facially younger than they are. She looked tired too, now that she wasn't shouting and laughing.

'Do you think so?' she asked. 'Well, maybe you're right. I never had time to stop and think about it. I've got a daughter, you see – she's forty now – got a congenital heart condition and they can't operate because she's got complicated blood. She's so frail I have to do nearly everything for her, bath her, get her on the lav, everything. It's hereditary. My husband died of it when she was three. She's a lovely girl but she can't really be left on her own for any length of time. Has blackouts, you see. I can't go out to work, never could, for that reason. That's why I started writing – used to do everything providing it would pay the bills, comics, horror stories, romances, thrillers. Then the editor of *Confessions* wrote and asked me to try my hand at Trues. Found I could do them a treat and they pay better than anything. Providing I can do my two Trues a week that brings me in enough to keep us both going.'

It was an appalling story – appalling and vulgar – like something out of a ghastly Victorian melodrama.

'I wouldn't be able to come here every year,' she wheezed on, 'if it wasn't for my sister. She comes and stays with Mary while I have this week. I love it. It's my holiday, party time. That's why I go a bit over the top sometimes, love. It has to do me for a whole year, see?'

I was glad when that week was over, even though I enjoyed my three gifted pupils. Mavis Ormitage began to tilt my sanity. When I went to bed at night I found pictures of her in my mind – propping her daughter up on cushions, bathing her, combing her hair, sitting at her typewriter pounding out those awful 'True Confessions'. I was, am, a very complete and fulfilled person, totally content with stretching my creativity to new boundaries. I was horrified with myself for allowing a monster like Mavis Ormitage to wreck my composure.

The week ended. I went home and in a few months almost forgot Mavis Ormitage. Louise Mitchell kept in touch with me. She sent me some of her work from time to time and although I don't usually give free advice to writers, I did think she was worth encouraging. I was sure that one day she was going to write something quite clever and innovative.

Three years later, in the hairdressers, I opened one of those glossy papers and found Louise Mitchell's face staring at me. She was sitting – carefully posed – on a Regency settee wearing a high-waisted, pink chiffon traily dress. The caption underneath said 'Historical Romantic Novelist, Louise Mitchell, hits the jackpot with her outrageous and imaginative sexy escapades. Louise proves that romance and steaming sex really do mix.'

There was a moment when I wanted to kill Louise Mitchell, tear that smug smiling face from the magazine and rip it into shreds. I felt betrayed, used. All the time she had been writing to me, sending me her little experimental pieces for my advice and criticism, she had been writing this bilge. I should have thrown the magazine away but I read on. Her latest advance was mentioned, $300,000 for the American rights and a film option taken out. This was her fifth book – somehow I'd missed the fact that she'd become a bestseller with the other four. I left the hairdressers and walked into the nearest bookshop and began to look at the popular paperback shelves, something I never, ever do. There they were, stacks of them, with gold lettering and crude illustrations. It was pathetic, ludicrous, hateful.

I couldn't sleep that night and I finally got up and wrote her a letter expressing just how deceitful and arrogant and unpleasant I thought her behaviour. I also added my views on the kind of garbage she was writing. I wrote six or seven versions of that letter, and in the end I sent none of them.

She must have known how I would feel because she stopped writing to me from that moment and when we found ourselves at a party given by the Society of Authors she looked straight at me without giving any indication that she knew me.

Last month I had a letter from Mr Bennett who runs the Writers' Summer School.

Dear Miss Cavendish,

It is some years since you took a creative writing course at our school and I wondered if you would be interested in coming to us again this year. The committee remembers your class with great interest. We didn't like to tell you at the time but we had never, at the school, had such a poorly-attended course as yours and that is why we dropped the experimental novel the following year. However, the passage of time has proved your course more productively rewarding than any of us envisaged.

Of course you know about Louise Mitchell who has become a household name and, it would appear, an extremely wealthy lady. You may perhaps *not* know about Cyril Biggs as his success is hidden under a pseudonym – Maxwell Lawrie! Yes, that's right. Cyril Biggs (who, loyal to the Summer School, came last year and took the espionage and thriller writers course) has become the creator of Vladimir Klein, international espionage agent.

You will find many old friends here to make you welcome at our jolly gatherings in the common room. Dear Mavis Ormitage is still to be with us but this will be a difficult year for her. Her daughter died at Christmas and I think her life will be very pointless without her. She will need her friends about her. Please let me know if you can take this year's course as soon as possible.

Best wishes,

Henry Bennett

As you know, taking a course at a writers' summer school is not something I would normally dream of doing, but I think perhaps I shall accept Mr Bennett's invitation this year. After all, the money is good and my last royalty cheque wasn't as large as it should have been. And maybe I can help one or two people to realise their full creative potential.

How Can a Cruise Be a Curse?

LISA ST AUBIN DE TERAN

Lisa St Aubin de Teran was born in 1953 in
South London. Her first novel *Keepers of the
House* (1982) won the Somerset Maugham
Award in 1983 and was runner-up for The
Guardian Fiction Prize. She is also the author of
four other highly acclaimed novels all published
by Jonathan Cape: *The Slow Train to Milan*
(1983); *The Tiger* (1984); *The Bay of Silence* (1986)
and *Black Idol* (1988). *The Marble Mountain and
Other Stories* was published by Jonathan Cape in
1989.

HOW CAN A CRUISE BE A CURSE?

How can a cruise be a curse? It's a nonsense really, and I wouldn't even think about it if it were not for Cyril going on and on. I have apportioned my life to suit my needs, dividing all that I have and consume. I had four children once: three pampered sons and a dusky love child. They are all gone. I never noticed them much while they were alive, except for the last one who crawled through my arteries leaving a trail of sun-sweat and linen. I loved my last child more than any other, but they were all equal in the eyes of God who chose to take them away. It was both the pound of flesh and a reminder that they were all equal. I have taken heed, and subsequently, whatever else may happen and wherever I may go, I divide all that I have and consume into quarter pounds. There is no posthumous neglect or favouritism. I remember them all. I have worshipped their memory at many altars, erecting as best I can a shrine to their four small crowns. But I think of them most since I began cruising, because we sail in and out of the hot zones of the Atlantic, and from Tenerife to Barbados and back the sultry afternoons are very like the ones spent in the big house before the hurricane came and swept it away. Except, of course, that I had servants then, so I never cleaned my own lavatories, and now I am the ladies' attendant.

There will be flying fish following our wake, there always are in the Caribbean, but I have little to do with the world of the decks, my world is down here, in the bowels off this ship, watering for the inner urgencies of passing strangers. I am given a post and a salary to do just that form of what I have always done. When the ship docks, and baskets of fresh fruit and vegetables are carried on board, bringing hidden lizards and geckos to crawl around the rails and floors, I confess that I feel a bit sad. People will flick the geckos into the sea. As the ship churns her way past the islands, little boys, and grown men too, will knock the lizards into the frothing waves beside us. When I sleep, I think of their small green bodies writhing in the ocean. It saddens me to feel them drowning because reptiles are a purer version of ourselves.

I have my own cupboard of supplies, and a set of scales. Whenever we dock at the port of La Coruna, I give my neighbour, Cyril Biggs, the money to buy scoops. I have brass and copper scoops, also one of engraved Toledo silver. Each one takes exactly 4 ozs of soap powder or 4 ozs of vim. But I still need the scales. I divide my days between scooping thus, cleaning, talking to Cyril and thinking about my newts. Perhaps I should say 'listening' to Cyril, since he has reached a point in his life when he is unable to contain his words; he is like a lavatory cistern that jams and overflows. His bitterness is seemingly uncontainable. His three cubicles are surrounded in mystery. The corners of his working space are unapproachable. He spends a great deal of his wages on two-tone shoes. He's really proud that they are made of real leather, but he won't wear them, they are just stacked in their cardboard boxes. They take up so much space now, Cyril can hardly move in there. When we're not talking, he strums out the devil's tattoo with his fingers on the partition wall. His side is covered with white tiles, and mine with mock pink marble, but neither of them make any difference, the thud and rhythm find their way through.

I have all that I want out of life, all that is available now that a pound of my flesh and my hopes are buried at the bottom of the sea. I have never lacked for company, and I am receptive to contacts as ephemeral as the passing of two masts in the night. Everyone who goes from the second class cabins to the dining room will pass my gangway, and, since ladies have weaker bladders than their escorts and more mirror addiction, they all come to me. Thousands of women have relieved themselves in my presence and pulled thousands more faces, straightened millions of hairs. I see the whole world funnelled down here.

Four years ago, I was offered the first class powder room, but I am happy here. I keep the end cubicle exclusively for my newts, where they are happy in its cistern. I have bred whole generations of salamanders there. I was once a lady of position myself, by which I mean merely that I too was rich in the wealth of paper and gold.

Much of those years was like sleepwalking. Occasionally I read books and magazines. I didn't have many books out there in the Tropics, it was an island for fruit and seafood, lobsters and limes, but I had a few: *A Room of My Own* and *Open Windows*. It was hot and close, and the cockroaches waited in lines like marching soldiers to invade the house. The windows were always open, but there were veils of stiff gauze over them to keep out the mosquitoes. My life was veiled there as well, except when the veil was torn and a young man crawled into me just the way that the old cook said the geckos would if she let them live.

The secret of life was somehow the room of my own. I have no need of villas or verandahs, I have my own room, the storeroom with more rolls of paper in it than there are bank rolls in a bank. So I am rich in my own currency. My guests are all transient. Some of them come on their passage from their cabins to the dining room, and some of them have come from snatched moments of pleasure in a rumpled bunk. Some of them come from the first class salons and have been taken short, wandering, and then return, because my cubicles are not just lavatories, they are an underwater world. There is a serenity about my domain. The scent of limes that I use to clean the mirrors wards off the nausea that catches people unawares at sea. Some people travel regularly on this ship, like the ballet dancer, Veronica what's-her'name? And there's the girl who calls herself a Jewish Princess, by which I suppose she means that she is very rich, who seems to have lived on the ship for the last two years. She lost her lover when she was still a girl and she seems to think that he will be able to find her here if she just follows a pattern of continual motion. She has green eyes, like my own love child, but there is none of the darkness in the creases of her skin nor the softness of lambs' wool hair.

When I first found this ship, I thought that I had discovered a secret haven. Now that I know it better, I realise that there are many people like me, healing their hearts and measuring their regrets here. We understand each other, we have no need to discuss the dinosaurs of our lost loves, their skeletons make themselves known by signs and hidden colours. We have our icons and our saints, and there are many unspoken words between us, many unfingered nerves. Every deck is criss-crossed with concealed frontiers. It is not hard to bear with all the torn emotions on board here because each voyage is of a limited duration and only a few of us will remain after the last island has been visited, and the last calypso sung. Those of us who choose to live here, cocooned by the rock and lull and the occasional lurch of this ocean liner, do so because it is good to live suspended between heaven and the sea's bed. Only Cyril is festering in his discontent.

He talks of other lives as though he were debarred from them. He has failed to see the freedom given to him by his space. He could be anyone or anything there in his cubicles, but he can think of nothing but the imaginary wrongs of his past. He calls his existence here a curse. He claims that it is a punishment for some earlier indiscretion. He tells me that he has bungled his life and forfeited his right to wear two-tone shoes. Sometimes I tell him just to put them on. All he has to do is kick off his scuffed and stained moccasins and slip into any pair of that new leather. He says he can't. He calls it destiny. He thinks he is doomed to have a greasy scalp and obliged to comb his balding hair across a scrofulous pate. I have given him sulphur weighed and measured by my own hand. I have given him shampoos of every kind and description. But it is impossible to get that man to wash his hair. I could communicate with my newts. I could make their salamander frills stand on their backs and blush with colour. I could make the old male turn around the cistern and climb up on the step cock and wave his transparent hand at me,

94

but I cannot find a shampoo that can turn back the stopped clock of Cyril's destiny.

He lives like a shrivelled Jeremiah through the wall. Every time he looks out through his porthole he mistakes the dense motion of the sea for the whirling of clouds. He believes that if he refrains from wearing his two-tone shoes he will, one day, be called back through the porthole and forgiven for whatever unmentionable thing it is that he has done. Meanwhile, he can't stop buying up the shoes, and although he has often told me that he really thinks it's a waste of my time to try and inculcate a sense of religion into my newts and that the shrine takes up a quarter of my ladies' room for nothing, he is blind to his own encroaching shoes.

Cyril assures me every time we set sail that we are heading towards our doom. He associates our ship with the Titanic, and although its course is far away from icebergs he is convinced that we shall sink and all be drowned. It is his favourite subject. He pretends that the mere mention of insurance policies is anathema to him, and yet, as though wound up by some invisible key, he will talk for hours about the pros and cons of this cover and that. It is not a subject that would normally spring to mind between one lavatory attendant and another, or even neighbours. However, Cyril has a compartment of his brain that navigates him through piles of policies whenever his mind strays from the possibilities of a holocaust.

I have had as many as sixteen newts at a time. Four-times-four is the perfect number for a colony. Had they all lived, they might have reinvented language. When I put my ear to the white porcelain of their tank I could hear music. Their hands were as soft and tender as my baby child's. At the time of the incident there were only seven. Seven is a number difficult to divide by four, but they were superior beings and therefore they were above my divisions. A fraction of their life fulfilled my own, so I knew they could have no need for my sums. Nobody except for Cyril and a girl called Ruth had ever seen them. Cyril was too pressed by his destiny to be impressed, but Ruth saw in them, as I had hoped she would, a source of hope and an escape from her voracious mother.

I always thought it a shame that Ruth's mother was not a man, she would have fared better with Cyril and his gloomy forebodings than anyone else I can think of. She needed to be reminded of time. She was a woman who had aged beyond her years while remaining as predatory as an adolescent. She also seemed incapable of movement without her daughter, Ruth, who lived a reluctant captivity by her side. They came to my cubicles more often than anyone else. The mother was obsessed by her makeup. She would spend hours smearing on layer after layer of gaudy paint, false eyelashes, fingernail extensions and knots of young bright hair. I understood her penchant for hairpieces. I have dyed my own hair many times. But there was a kind of desperation about her search for sexual adulation. She was blind to herself, blind when she looked in the mirror and failed to see the raddled creature staring back at her, and she was blind to her plight and blind to the ridicule of all who saw her. I often wondered if she and Cyril, should they both drop their disguises, could be happy together. Maybe not, she was too intent on happiness to find any and Cyril was too intent on despair.

Be that as it may, on the afternoons when Ruth was able to slip away from her mother, she would come and talk to me in the ladies', whispering her crushed American dreams to me as she lamented her predicament, her mother's nymphomania and her wish to learn the newt language that alone kept me so calm. My life was like a rainbow that has come full circle. My feelings were stretched and tuned like the arc of a bow. The droning of Cyril's voice and tapping fingers became like a muffled percussion to the finer melodies that flowed from the reptilian cistern. In fact, my life would have been quite perfect were it not for the incident. And the incident I confess was foretold by my prophetic neighbour long before it occurred.

I have never been clairvoyant, but I should have guessed as anyone might that all was not well on our gangway, the day that the four horsemen of the Apocalypse came striding by. I was standing in the doorway of my storeroom, dividing the soap powder with my silver scoop, when they passed. Three of them were wearing full-length black coats and black hats, and they looked identical with their ashen faces and their dark ringlets hanging by their ears. They advanced in a very menacing way and invaded Cyril's space. The fourth man who was with them defies description. I cannot say whether he was fair or dark. I cannot recall whether he too wore a long black coat. All I know is that as they passed I felt a chill fill the corridor and I waited for them to come out of the gents' with such concentration that I was only half aware of the events that led up to the incident.

There were only three cubicles there, and no urinal, because Cyril's shoes had long since blocked all that. No sound of flushing came from there, nor any sound at all. I know that the incident occurred at three o'clock in the afternoon, and I can vouch that the three Jews and their companion did not leave Cyril's room between then and ten o'clock that evening. Whether they strode away during the sixteen minutes of my absence when I stalked the fat woman to the upper deck, I do not know. They could have disappeared while I crept up behind the whale-blubber back of the offender. They were not on the top deck as her pear-shaped hips tumbled over and over to the water. There was no-one there but me. I'm quite sure of that. I heard, later, that she was famous. Apparently, people had been going up to her during the voyage to get her signature. I don't suppose the fish would be too interested in her career, but then, they too are a superior species. They would appreciate the fat woman for her worth. Their lips would kiss her white flesh in a different way. There must be a strand of justice in it somewhere.

No-one had ever gone into my locked cubicle before. It wasn't a strong lock, it never had to be. There was an unwritten code on the ship, a respect for all our loves and eccentricities. It was a space partitioned into spaces each allotted to someone for the duration of the voyage. We accepted our reliance on numbers there, and the presence of the sea below us had a salutary effect.

There were four cubicles in my ladies' room. One more than Cyril's because we women are renowned for our mirror work and the weakness of our bladders. There were three cubicles open and available to the fat pretender when she barged into my kingdom. It is obvious, though, that despite her seemingly straight posture she was weighed down on one side by greed. She needed all that was not hers. The four horsemen had announced her coming. The rest she did herself. Even the food in her guts was not the food of other mortals. She was rotting with the richness of it all. She threw herself into my space and her fatness filled my world, then she burst into my shrine and exploded over the bowl. Only Cyril and Ruth

and myself had ever been close to my newts. We understood their superiority and we worshipped them. Perhaps
in the case of Cyril I should say that it was merely respect.
There is no name for the sacrilege that the fat woman
committed. She had names, apparently, for her bestsellers
and for all the fat characters who swelled their covers, but
what she did have no one word can describe; I know her
name, but I ignore it. I shall not pronounce the syllables
of the person who filled my inner chamber with diarrhoea
and then flushed the chain on the greatest colony of newts
I have ever seen.

Cyril warned me. He often said all that was good and
fine would be washed into the sea and drowned. Our
communion would be only with fishes, and dead things
and dinosaurs' bones. He claimed that our very presence
there under the water was a portent of our eventual ruin.
I would have rather died myself in that warm salt water
of the Caribbean than have lost my salamanders so. I
would have gladly died in their stead. I think of them
gasping in the brine and it fills my head with nightmares.
The fact that the assassin has joined her victims is merely
a link in the chain, it hasn't returned my darlings to me.
Sometimes, even more than their melodies, I miss the
tiny grip of their fingers.

It takes sixteen days to cross the Atlantic from Southampton to Barbados, calling at La Coruna and Tenerife.
We are weaving a tapestry with our sea tracks. I have
begun to wonder whether salamander newts can, despite
all the evidence to the contrary, survive away from fresh
water. Perhaps, instead of drowning, they merely evolved
in their new saline environment. Perhaps, being a superior
species, they have developed talents beyond my imagin-
ings and have founded a colony far down on the sea-bed.

99

The Royal Spread

MARY FLANAGAN

Mary Flanagan was born in New England. She was educated by the Sisters of Mercy and at Brandeis University where she received a degree in History of Art. She lived a year in Morocco then emigrated to England in 1969. In 1984 she published *Bad Girls*, a collection of short stories. *Trust*, her first novel, appeared in 1987. Both books have been translated into several languages. She now lives in London where she is at work on another novel.

THE ROYAL SPREAD

'First still your mind. It's important to have a serious attitude. Notice how the room is free of distracting influences: only dark colours, no bright lights, no next-door conversations, no music or animals, no open windows. The phone's off the hook, so just relax and concentrate.

'Today we're using the Royal Spread, so I am removing – are you watching? – the twenty-four cards numbered five through ten in each of the four suits. To what remains we will add the Major Arcana and the Court Cards from which I want you to select one to represent yourself, the questioner. This is the Key Card.'

She was very thin, no bigger than a twelve-year-old. The large mahogany chair on which she perched exaggerated her fragility. Her silver-blonde hair was done up in a bouffant set precariously above a face like an ageing child's. Her eyes were bright and efficient. The nails of her little hands were painted a deep cerise and her feet nestled in tiny silver slippers. She had a doctor's brisk manner. On the wall behind her was a large drawing of concentric circles in white, black and amber with Hebrew letters orbiting the perimeter. Beside her was an unfinished bowl of rice pudding.

'Would you like some help, Isabel?'

I nodded.

'Well, let's see. Remember that the four suits are equivalent to the elements fire, air, earth and water. You're dark but not too, with green eyes. That's Pentacles. They're not as dark as Swords. Wands of course are very fair people, Scandanavian types and redheads, Cups less fair. Men choose Kings, Knights or Pages to represent themselves, women Queens or Princesses who are actually Pages, I know it's confusing. How do you feel?'

'Not very much like a Queen.' I was nervous and in a hurry for the answer to my question. I had waited a long time to see Ruth Church, the Australian clairvoyante.

'Right. Princess of Pentacles for you.' She placed the Key Card in the middle of the table. 'The Princess has a desire for knowledge. She is primarily reflective but is capable of great dedication. She has a good heart but is inclined to melancholy. She also has a rebellious streak and sometimes fails to see the obvious.'

How could she know that?

'Now hold the deck in both hands and think about this: the Tarot is a sacred book, ancient as Egypt. The cards tell an eternal story. I call this story that has no end the divine plot. The images work on our unconscious. Shuffling establishes a rapport between them and the questioner. Concentrate. The cards never lie.'

At her instructions, I shuffled then riffled the pack.

'Everything before the Key Card is past. The following cards will tell us the consequences of what has gone before.'

She laid out the deck in the shape of a Celtic cross. She spread my life before me, reading it from the top row down and from right to left. The pictures were like a troupe of actors appearing one by one before a spotlight then grouping to form tableaux vivants.

'The subject of your question is the Knight of Cups. He is the beloved, the lover. A young man with curly brown hair, a romantic fond of poetry and music, indolent but enthusiastic if roused. Often idealistic with high aspirations. Very receptive, though a slave to feeling. Very kind.'

And with his kindness, Carlos took away my weapons and left me with not one defence against him. I had come here disarmed, hoping for a clue to his whereabouts.

He was my secret, my treasure, my bane. I marked him out as holy that first morning I met him in the kitchen. I watched him set down a box of groceries containing pickled ginger, blini mix, fresh pasta, honey from Hymettus and tropical fruits. He was the new delivery boy from Daleth Foods. A lime fell out of the box and rolled across the black and white tiled floor. We both hastened to pick it up and stopped short of collision, poised like two dancers. He handed me the fruit.

'Thank you,' I said. And then, because I was nervous, 'I love limes.'

He too loved them. They reminded him of the island on which he'd grown up. He was the son of an obscure Spanish composer, and his family had led a nomadic existence. Immediately I began to weave fantasies around him, with threads and nets and webs to ensnare only myself. I fed upon his presence and upon everything he told me.

He had run away from the army and was living under an assumed name. He played the electric violin in a group called The Saints who performed in small clubs and occasionally on cruises. He loved music and freedom and despised money. He saw no need to live normally.

'The King of Pentacles: a rich man, a successful man, reliable in marriage, clever but limited, with an ability to acquire money and a love of valuable possessions. When betrayed he is capable of any excess to achieve his end. A suspicious and dangerous man.'

A man built to last. My husband. Older than I. The head of an insurance firm. Because I had been suitably docile he was kind to me. Until now in his jealousy he put out antennae omniscient as an insect's.

'The High Priestess. A wise woman. That's me for sure. I'm not reversed, you see. I'm upright, and next to the Chariot, also upright. I can help you, so follow my advice. The High Priestess is hidden behind a veil, and she communicates her knowledge to very few. For you I am a true medium. So pay attention if you want to find this boy.

'Oh-oh. The Page of Swords, and reversed. Watch out for him, young lady. He's a spy. He is vigilant and discreet and busy in mischief. He is in the pay of the King of Pentacles and will be revealed as an impostor.

'Now this one,' she tapped the card with her sharp red nail, 'is really interesting. He's the Magician, someone from whom you can learn a great deal. A clever, dextrous person. He is a conjuror with many tricks. He too enjoys a disguise at your expense. Don't be distracted. Watch what he does and respect him. He has a superior intellect, though he will have his little jokes. He seems to be closely allied to the Empress: creative aspect of the feminine. She presides over a door which is the gateway to the watery element. See how her throne rests on the sea from which she herself arose, like Venus. Look for her there. She is a beautiful matron, but also, like you, a daughter.'

I thought of my mother who had run away when I was in my teens. From time to time she wrote to me, but I hadn't heard from her in two years. In her last letter she said, 'Never have an affair with a musician.' I had forgotten her advice, and now I had only the High Priestess to help me.

'The Ace of Wands indicates a new undertaking. You will make an important change but it will cost you plenty – '

(I could easily imagine what it would cost me.)

'– because here we have the Tower, a catastrophic card. You will be blasted by lightning and topple from a high place. But remember that, for some, destruction can be a liberating influence.'

She rested her hands on the edge of the table and leaned towards me. 'Your search is mad, my dear, but it is not in vain. The next client is waiting. Bye for now.'

I paid her and left. That was the last I saw of Mrs Church and her wicked pack of cards.

Or perhaps not. There was that time on the *Cybele*. I thought I saw her with the three Jews, dressed like them in black, her face partially covered by a hat with a veil. She strode the decks beside them, a small malevolent bird of prey. I was not the only passenger to retreat to my cabin rather than pass them in the halls. Then the incident occurred. It unnerved me so badly that I was tempted to abandon my search and go home, a repentant wife. I nearly forgot that I was the Princess of Pentacles and must play my part.

When I first met Carlos I was pale and mute and wandered about like the heroine of a Bulwer Lytton novel. I was afraid he would despise me for the wealthy indentured wife I was. But he swore it didn't matter. He was genuinely in love with me, I'm sure of it. When we were not together I locked myself in my room and smoked and listened to music late into the night. I was happy.

Then I received a letter saying that he was afraid the

army had discovered his whereabouts. He was leaving immediately and would write. Incautious with grief, I rang Daleth Foods where a man with an Eastern European accent informed me that he knew of no Carlos Mompou.

I went to the club where he sometimes played with The Saints. They said maybe he had gone back to his island. Maybe he would earn his passage by entertaining on cruise ships. Maybe he was hiding right here in the city. They didn't trust me, and why should they? Me in my designer suit that fitted like a second skin, my reptile shoes and bag. I knew I must abandon all that.

I went home and packed a suitcase with only a few of my oldest clothes, wrote a note to my husband and left by way of the private park behind our house. I made one stop at Cronos Bookshop where I purchased a deck of cards. Then I went to a travel agent and booked a passage on the *Cybele*. I spent the next few days in a cheap hotel playing with the cards and sleeping under my cloak which is the colour of the southern sea. The following week I took Mrs Church's advice and went searching for Carlos on the water.

I worried that my husband would follow me. I had said in the note that I could not explain my action, although he probably guessed. He would never understand the real reasons for my leaving – that Carlos's idealism had shamed and inspired me, that I envied him his poverty and that I wanted to be rid of the expensive clutter my husband used to insulate us from the outside world. I was tired of security and good taste and of being a prisoner of money which is all, always, tainted. That is why I shed the raiments which others hold in such esteem. I no longer wished to be a walking incitement to envy. I wanted to be like the Knight of Cups whose aspirations are so dizzyingly high. I made many journeys before I found him.

It was on the final cruise when I met the kind though clearly unbalanced attendant of the ladies' washroom. Our Lady of the Lavatory they called her. I introduced myself as the Princess of Pentacles, and she was not in the least alarmed. I asked her about Carlos, and though she did not know him personally, she had heard of The Saints, which I took as confirmation that I had not imagined this story.

'They played here once,' she said, staring at me from behind large pink-rimmed spectacles that magnified her already myopic eyes. She had an impressive dignity. She had been beautiful, you could tell.

I told her how I had forgotten then ignored my mother's warning never to have an affair with a musician and how I was following the advice of Mrs Church.

'The cards are only a game,' she said, 'like Consequences. Every quest is really a longing to know what lies behind the surface of things.'

'How can I find that out?'

'Ask the Jewish grocers.' She retreated to her cubicle and locked the door. We did not speak again, and when the boat docked a week later she disappeared in mysterious circumstances.

When you are alone in the world and you speak to no-one every encounter becomes highly charged and unbearably significant. You become aware that each person, each object carries its own awful import.

The only Jews I could assume she meant were the three on the cruise. I waited outside their door, hoping for a word with them, but they eluded me. Sometimes I could hear them speaking in what sounded like Hebrew but they managed to come and go without my catching them.

I made enquiries and was told that they were the Moses Brothers who owned and ran Daleth Foods. I knew then that the Jews held all or part of the secret. I was determined to penetrate their disguise and to invade their cabin sanctuary.

One morning I saw them standing by the railing watching the flying fish that followed the wake of the ship. I went immediately to the lower deck and tried the door to their room but of course it was locked. I waited in the shadows, knowing this would be my only chance. The maid arrived with fresh linen and an assortment of mops, brushes and chemicals. I slipped in behind her and hid in the closet until she had finished. I am a thief, I thought, a thief and a spy. That did not stop me from groping in the semi-darkness at their strange belongings, looking for I didn't know what.

All the maid's cleaning agents had not eradicated the smell, both stifling and seductive, of mouldy paper and decaying leather bindings. My hands encountered stacks of books which I carried to the porthole, the better to squint at the lettering on their ancient covers. The *Zohar*, the *Sepher Yetzirah*, the *Sepher Ha Bahir*. I took them, along with a few others, leaving behind all those written in Hebrew. On my way to the door, I could not resist another look in the closet. There among the black coats and shoes and trousers was a silver-blonde wig.

They knew where Carlos was, I had no doubt. It was my plan to approach them as an acolyte and beg them to tell me not only his whereabouts but the secret of what lay behind the appearance of things. Love, no matter how base, always leads us to our higher selves.

Often I feared reprisals. Surely they, in their sagacity, could easily determine who was responsible for the theft. But once I commenced reading the purloined books, anxiety was burnt away in the fire of my imagination. I spent the last two days of the journey locked in my room under my blue cloak, too enthralled to sleep or eat. Through the maid word reached me of the incident, and in my febrile state I assumed that the fat woman, whom everyone seemed to know, was the innocent victim of a punishment which only I deserved. Still, I read on.

When we docked, I went to a small hotel and read some more. The oppressive heat, the flies and the lizards were powerless to distract me. Three weeks passed, and I realised I had not even bothered to look for Carlos. The next day I left on the *Cybele*, assuming from what I had seen of the passenger list that the genies in black would again by my shipmates. But I found their cabin occupied by an ex-tennis player. I looked for the solemn keeper of the ladies' washroom, hoping she might enlighten me, but she too was gone.

I went next door to make enquiries at the men's lavatory, but the attendant said that the ship was doomed and asked if I had a good insurance policy. I ran out, tripping over a pair of two-toned shoes. Only later did I realise he reminded me of someone.

I could not return home, I had not found Carlos, and the magicians had eluded me. Mrs Church had been right. My quest was mad. I began to wonder who the dealer might be in this game. Sometimes I wondered if I had ever met Carlos.

I travelled to a northern city, bought some more books on the Kabbalah and read on. When winter came I moved south, earning my living by waitressing in cafés or washing dishes. I wanted, beyond anything, to be obscure. I saved my money for books and for a return trip to the island.

I sacrificed, I studied, I followed the path of severity. I

learned that before the world was made there were twenty-two letters of pure light and that these devolved into matter. I learned of the Four Worlds and the Conjuration of the Four; the Abyss of Daath, the Three Supernals, the Prayer of the Salamanders. I read of the Mystical Marriage and of the Bride of Microprosopus who is the Lesser Countenance. I knew the significance of Tetragrammaton and measured out my life in fours. I was engrossed in an impossible plot in which all the characters were abstract qualities, formless monuments that marked the stages of an interior journey. I saw a vast classification system in which all phenomena might be filed. I learned that everything was alive with meaning. I knew also that I was only the Princess of Pentacles, inhabiting the realm of Malkuth which is weighed down by gravity and visibleness.

Years passed, perhaps not years. I counted time, as well as coffee and sugar, in different units than before. When I was ready at last I left my job, packed my books, put on my blue cloak which was now ragged and dirty, and returned to the city where my husband lived and where I had met Carlos and begun my search for him. I went straight to Daleth Foods.

I stood outside the shop holding my suitcase which was heavy with the occult. They had been waiting for me, I knew. They wanted to listen. I would show them what I had accomplished with the treasure they had unwittingly loaned me. The bell above the door tinkled as I entered.

'Good morning,' someone said, although it was late afternoon. Slowly my eyes adjusted to the semi-darkness. The three Jews stood behind the counter wearing white aprons. A woman waited by the check-out with a pile of small purchases – pickled ginger, roseate pasta, honey, rice pudding. She reminded me of my mother. Beside her was a young girl who talked incessantly in an inaudible voice. The woman did not seem to be listening. She stared at me from behind large pink glasses that magnified the pupils and all the puckery lines around her once-beautiful eyes.

Nothing stirred. There was no sound except for the muttering of the girl. We all stood immobile like actors in a tableau vivant. Then a young man entered with some boxes which he set down in the corner opposite me. I could not see his face, but noticed the soft brown hair that curled over the back of his neck. He turned and met my eyes. It was then that reality slipped past itself like two panes of oiled glass. One cannot look into the face of God and live.

I woke up walking the streets in another part of the city. My suitcase had become so heavy I was unable to go a step further, and I sat down to rest on a bench next to a railing that surrounded a private park. Beside me was a telephone booth where a man was having a conversation. When I tried to reassemble the scene in the shop, all I could conjure was the indecipherable speech of the girl. I panicked. I would return tomorrow. No, I would return now and wait all night outside the door of Daleth Foods.

I took a deep breath and reached for my bag. Suddenly there was a hand on my shoulder. Then two men were guiding me towards a waiting car. My husband drove. I sat in the back with the man from the telephone booth who kept a tight hold on my arm. He bragged to my husband about how he had followed me and caught me at last.

'We all know what we do best,' he said.

When we passed under streetlight I looked down and saw his feet. I knew who was the Page of Swords, the Spy.

The keepers of the Tower will not allow me my precious books which they say are responsible for my illness. I have begged the keepers to return them to the Jews but they take no notice. Whenever my husband visits me – he is my only visitor – he insists that this is a hospital. Over and over he insists upon this. He thinks that reason is a weapon for good. At least they have let me keep the pack of cards. They regard it as an amusement, a harmless game to while away the time which they measure in ordinary units. They have no way of knowing how well this place suits my purpose.

A locked room is perfect for stilling the mind. The quiet is conducive to concentration. Here there are no distracting influences – no bright lights or overheard conversations, no telephones, no music or animals, no open windows. I hold the deck in my hands, intent upon the oracle. I select a Key Card and place it before me. I extract the cards numbered five through ten from each of the four suits. I shuffle then riffle the pack, allowing my unconscious to establish a rapport with the cards. I lay them all out in the shape of a Celtic cross. I look at them for a long time. Then reading from top to bottom, from left to right, I let them tell me this story.

In the Scheme of Things

MARINA WARNER

Marina Warner is a writer of fiction, history and criticism. Born in London in 1946, and educated at Lady Margaret Hall, Oxford, she is the author of three praised studies of mythology: *Alone of All Her Sex: the myth and cult of the Virgin Mary*, *Joan of Arc: the image of female heroism*, and *Monuments and Maidens: the allegory of the female form* (winner of the Fawcett Prize, 1986). She has published three novels, *In a Dark Wood*, *The Skating Party*, and *The Lost Father* which was shortlisted for the Booker Prize in 1988. She lives in London, is working on a study of the fairytale, and is writing a new novel.

IN THE SCHEME OF THINGS

Five years of catastrophes, but the ruler had held the nation together. He wasn't to blame, not for the visitations of fate on his country. It wasn't within his power to descry the writing of destiny before it appeared on the wall. He wasn't one of those old-fashioned despots, after all, who presumed to know the mind of the Almighty and employed priests to read signs, in knucklebones or the entrails of animals. This was the twentieth century, and he knew man's place in the scheme of things, and so did his people. They didn't expect him to conjure order from chaos, to set against the dealings of fortune the petty strength of the human hand. But they were grateful, very grateful, for his providence and understanding. Without him, the condition of the people would be far worse. No, they didn't blame him, they didn't blame him at all.

The disasters had been untoward, it had to be admitted. No-one had ever heard of such plagues before, in such quick succession, at least not since Yahweh blasted the Egyptians, as the rabbis were quick to point out. Those grocers in the Jewish quarter pointed the finger at him, their ruler, he knew it, much more readily than other sections of his community, who loved him. They saw a connection between the chain of catastrophes and his dispensation. They called him *Pharaoh*.

The ruler ground his teeth and bunched his fist at the thought, and decided he would command the palace chef to stop buying from them, even though Estella, his daughter, liked the almond biscuits they baked and their squid's ink pasta (sable-black ringlets with a caviare flavour) more than anything in the world, or so she said.

Looking back, he supposed that the catastrophes had begun in his first year of office, when the library in the main square caught fire one night and the conflagration spread through Foreign Literature in Translation, Social & Political Science, and had begun to consume History, before the firemen got the blaze under control. He visited the scene the next day, and made a public statement of mourning for the hundreds of years' collections of destroyed knowledge. His nose was still filled with the sharp scent of burned books. Curious, he had thought, it was almost an organic smell, almost fragrant, like roasting meat.

They never found a culprit. The ruler had directed the public inquiry to search among the literary community. It was bound to be one of them who'd set the fires, he told the tribunal in confidence. Writers were an unstable, envious lot. And even if you kept them corralled into writers' colonies, as he tried to do, giving them every opportunity and privilege of practising their craft securely, you couldn't be sure you'd caught every one.

But the police hadn't come up with a guilty party, unfortunately, though they'd detained a strong suspect for a while, and nearly achieved a confession. A novelist. The ruler sighed, and wrote a memo to himself to ask the Chief of Police about the last writers' tally. He hoped the number of writers was decreasing. Else he might have to take further action.

After the library fire, the next disaster had been – he pondered a while, it was easy to confuse the chronology – yes, that was it, another fire, this time in the shafts bringing the mint workers up from the bullion vaults. That was a strange one: thirty-five dead and several others so badly burned they would have to wear surgical masks until the skin grafts could be done. And there was a waiting-list. It seemed someone had chucked out a cigarette on stepping into the lift, and the litter at the bottom of the shaft had caught alight. Only a bonfire, really, but it had burned through the cable and brought the cage crashing down. Then the rescue work – well, it turned out that the emergency stairs hadn't been used for a while, and the maintenance had been neglected. . . . The ruler dismissed the thought – it was distressing him, to no purpose.

Think of the natural disasters instead, he admonished himself. Look on the bright side, as his mother used to tell him. Turn your mind to the calamities for which nobody could possibly be responsible: don't think of the shipwreck, when the boat slewed round, filling with water at its rear end until it pitched over and plunged the passengers into the winter sea. Don't consider the airbus that lost a wing over the chief city of the inner plain, or the street sliced through by the giant wing as it careened down to earth followed by the broken fuselage. Or the small plane that exploded . . . or the trains that collided and in the impact passed clean over one another, like coupling rhinos. No, he scolded himself, a gloomy outlook will not do.

He had always held to a strictly materialist view, according to the principles of his upbringing, but these

days he began to feel stirrings of sympathy with the growing number among his subjects who believed in a dangerous malign force at work. Perhaps after all, someone was
to blame, someone busy undermining the central power,
his own righteous authority. There were some among his
people who were becoming impatient with his scepticism,
who clamoured that divine vengeance was behind the
disasters, and would increase in vigour until it was recognised and given due worship. Some religious groups clamoured for expiation, urging their ruler to recognise the
close battle joined on earth between the powers of darkness and of light and to root out the wicked. He wouldn't
have paid attention to them in old, secular times, but he
had to watch the direction of the wind if he were to fulfil
his promise as a good ruler. The faithful were prone to
point a finger at the wicked. Who knows who they might
finger next. The ruler grasped his pen and began writing
a memo to the Chief of Police. He must have these new
fanatics watched too, before they overtook him in his
plans. Perhaps there was a grain of truth to what they
said, that God has his own ways; that there's a hidden
meaning to his plans. He sends trials to test us.

Like the sudden plague of leeches: it had become difficult, in his kingdom, to go for a walk without finding
one of the creatures or more fastened to one's flesh, bur-
rowing in at both ends, it seemed, liquid patent-leather
curls squirming for a good grasp. They'd been known in
the country, for a while, of course, and country people
knew to look out for them, examine themselves carefully
coming in from the outdoors, in the creases and folds of
flesh – small children were especially vulnerable – but
since last year, the problem had arrived in the cities.

And now there was this flower that had sprung up
among the crops, a beautiful thing, Asiatic witchweed,

the botanists called it, with a translucent purple corolla
and scarlet stamens. It could reduce a crop to chaff within
a week: leaving fields luxuriantly ablaze with colour and
no harvest. He had called his agricultural physicists to
analyse the prodigy immediately. They had reported back
that the flower had no root: that it blew through the air
and plugged itself into whatever host it could find, corn
or barley or oats, whatever, and that it simply could adapt
itself to suit. It was like the best of guests, at home
anywhere, in any company, at any function; and they
could think of nothing to stop its continuing triumphant
conquest of their society's food supply.

So when the salamanders were washed up on the beach
down by the coastguard station, most witnesses were
relieved they were dead. That they weren't capable of
breeding anymore, of infesting the countryside and the
cities and duplicating themselves with green scaly pro-
geny. They lay on the shingle, their scalloped ruffs closed
like broken umbrellas, their iridescent scales dull and
rimmed with salt, their tails loose as the wrack on the
highwater; they looked like so many dragons eviscerated
by Saint George. Though the stench was overpowering,
the people swarmed down to the water's edge to look at
them; some poked with a foot at the heap of dead reptiles,
others stood, holding their noses, and kept their distance.
A man kicked over a head, to look into the pale green
snout of the salamander, and its veined eyelids, lying over
sunken eyeballs, were as translucent as new beech leaves
in summer. Another poked at the carcass of a big brute,
and as its foreleg, crowned with claws, rose up under the
prodding boot and fell back, a shudder ran through the
crowd.

Then there was a stir in the jetsam, the flick of a tail
on the shingle and one beast raised his head from among

his drowned companions and swung it slowly from side to side, pulling one leg from the tangled bodies, then another, as he lifted himself upright again.

Some people in the crowd shrieked; the children cringed into the shelter of the nearest adult, but thrilled, breathless with anticipation, clinging on in order to prevent the retreat up the beach that had begun. But when the salamander first opened its dark mouth, the spectators couldn't be restrained, certainly not by children. At the sight of the long, slender, black tongue whipping from side to side like a fisherman playing a salmon, a howl went up and the crowd broke up. Some scrambled back to the promenade above the beach, mobbing the narrow steps; they were screaming when they could not make headway, and they squeezed up so tight that the older people present were carried by the momentum of the crush and would have been trampled if they had fallen. Others rushed the animal as it lumbered up the shingle towards them and fanned out around it to head it off.

'Drive it back!'

'Hold it down!'

'This way!'

'No, this way!'

Some yarrupped and clicked at the beast, as it stepped clumsily one way then the other in confusion.

'Into the sea – drown the monster!'

The salamander was still dazed from his passage in the cold ocean and the exposure to horror he had endured: he had known nothing like it in his earlier existence, not even in the cramped ship's cistern, let alone the baked desert where he had been captured originally by a specimen hunter. Faced with the jeering, menacing ring of men and women who were picking up stones and throwing them at him to force him back into the horrible cold ocean he had so miraculously survived, the beast summoned up all his powers: he stood fast beneath the assault, the pebbles falling harmlessly off his green scales which were beginning to glow again with defiant rage. As he stood there taking their blows, the people saw his tail stiffen with muscle, its forked end spark with fire where it lashed the beach, his frilled wings spread like a swan's, his neck arch and his emerald ruff rise in points to make an aureole around his head; now the tongue darted back and forth among the flames that flickered in the air before him. Though he had inflated his size to full fighting panoply, he was still much smaller than his assailants.

The stoners faltered. The impression he made was of a much bigger creature, and one growing more huge by the minute. Some held back through fear; others began to cry out in wonder. At the back a child was wailing, 'They're going to kill him; they're going to kill him' over and over.

Then one of the most enthusiastic stoners dropped his arm and shouted, 'Take him to the Ruler! Let him decide!'

Others took up the cry, and dropped their missives and began making googoo noises and cluckings in their throats, to bring the animal to heel. But he continued to stand his ground, unmoved, swaying his long neck and flicking the black cord of his tongue into the flames hissing from his jaws and nostrils, until the police arrived with a net of a fine metal wire and threw it over him and pulled the drawstring tight and then dragged him up the ramp used for launching the lifeboat (in the days when there had been a lifeboat and volunteers to crew it) and left him on the broadwalk above the beach, near the bandstand until the ruler could come and decide his fate.

Estella was with her father when the news of the beast's

miraculous survival and his strange qualities was brought to the palace.

'It's an omen, Daddy, an evil omen,' she said, plaintively. 'Another one.'

'*We* don't believe in omens, darling.' But to his daughter, his tone was indulgent. 'We leave that to the superstitious, to little-minded people, who find significance in everything and fear it.'

He wanted her to come with him, but she wouldn't. Estella did not add that she had a feeling about the beast, that it was destined for her, that something out of the sea was seeking her out, specially, and she was scared. He cajoled her, and when she still wouldn't, he made her. He could not have his only child fearful as a peasant before random, meaningless prodigies.

The police chief had ordered the disposal of the corpses on the tideline; the reptiles were being burned on the shore and the reek was appalling.

As they approached the trapped animal, they could hear him howling through the hiss of his flaming breath. When they stood by, they watched him flail in the net for a few moments. The princess covered her face with her sleeve. Her father then gave the order, 'Bring it to the palace. Alive.'

As he turned away, the policeman, wearing riot gear, positioned themselves around the thrashing animal before they closed in.

'I want you to have it, my darling, as a present,' the ruler said when the salamander was brought to the palace. 'It'll make a pet fit for a Queen!' He thought it very funny when his daughter turned pale at the gift.

The salamander's jaws were muzzled and his claws had been clipped by the police surgeon. 'It'll make a splendid guard dog, you'll see. The fire-eating'll stop, as soon as it's used to its new surroundings. It'll learn which side its bread is buttered soon enough!' And the ruler roared with laughter.

When her father laughed, there was no point arguing. Estella took the leash the police officer handed to her, and murmured something by way of thanks.

'What's that you say?' he shouted, and slapped his thigh with delight as she led the beast off to her quarters. 'She'll soon see. Nothing can scare me, nor the flesh of my flesh. She'll learn. Nothing.'

For some time, Estella couldn't bring herself to look at the beast. She put him in an old fish tank she had and agreed to keep a light on to keep him warm after one of her maids told her salamanders needed heat. She called the girl in, since she seemed to have a way with animals, when the creature needed to have its muzzle off to eat and drink. But she couldn't bear to hear it feed, prolonging its hateful life. She wanted to wake up one morning and find the salamander dead.

One afternoon, as the sun moved round with the lengthening days, the beam reached the tank where the salamander was confined, and she found herself watching him bask. The green scales glowed in the light, flecks glancing off their scalloped edges. She became curious and approached the small dragon-like creature in her keeping, and put out her hand to the flames in his breath. She found that his fire was pleasant to the touch, like a warmed stone. She tried again, reached out farther and a flame curled around her fingers, sending delicious shivers through her. The black tongue followed, wrapped itself around her wrist and filled her with a melting, fainty feeling she had not ever known before. She cried out, softly, and reached to fondle the creature's head. Again the flames flushed her with pleasure and the tongue's movement made her tingle. She reached into the fish tank and picked up the salamander and gently set him down.

'Let's go for a walk,' he said. 'I need some fresh air.'

They walked. Now she found something magnificent in his step, in the green fan of his ruff and the heavy somnolence of his long neck and tail. She skipped to keep up with him, feeling like a little girl beside him, being shown the world for the first time.

On that day, and day after day after that, for as long as happiness was allowed them, they explored, first the palace gardens, then the country beyond. She walked in the chief city of her father's realm for the first time without ceremonial attendants. She spoke to strangers.

Together, they found secret places where they could lie down. In an orchard one day, they curled together under the apple tree and the blossoms fell on them like wedding confetti. She couldn't believe that she had once found him ugly, or that she had feared him. His body was more beautiful to her now than anything she had known, and the touch of his breath on her skin made her quiver inside.

Their conversations were long, intense, filled with anxieties and punctuated with laughter. Sometimes, they quarrelled: the privilege that she had always enjoyed occasionally made her touchy, when she saw he was horrified by her ignorance. Sometimes, the pleasure that they could give each other made them want to test their powers of resistance, and the boundaries of their dominion over each other. She came to trust him and, with that trust, she discovered many things about herself and her feelings she had not been able to voice before. She saw now how people were suffering under her father. How many hundreds of people had mysteriously disappeared, her own mother among them. How the accidents that had befallen the kingdom weren't meaningless, as her father the ruler always maintained.

'Be careful, my love,' said the beast, when she confided in him her new, disturbing thoughts.

'But there is such a thing as responsibility,' she cried. 'Fate can't be made to blame for everything.'

Estella couldn't altogether believe that her father was blind to the discoveries she had made, for they now seemed to her glaringly obvious.

'I was thinking, Daddy,' she said, as they were talking together one evening, after dinner. 'Couldn't we declare a national day of mourning, for my mother and for all the others who've disappeared no-one knows where? Like armistice day, when everyone could wear flowers in commemoration of the fallen. White violets – they were her favourite flower, I remember.'

The ruler was eating a peach. It went sideways. When he'd stopped choking, he asked Estella,

'Who's been putting such ideas in your pretty little head?'

'I can think for myself, you know,' she said. 'I'm growing up.'

Another evening, she suggested, 'You know the inquiry into the library burning? Don't you think it could be reopened? I mean, it is terrible we lost all those books, and really, Daddy, no stone should be left unturned, don't you think?' In her teens, she was acquiring a rather imperious manner, like a princess in a fairytale.

Her father had her maids questioned. No, she was seeing no-one. She spent all her days with the salamander, wandering the gardens. They never let her out of their sight, they assured him. She was blissfully happy, nobody who attended her had ever seen her so rosy, so alert, so eager to begin the day and so fulfilled at its close. She slept easy, and her dreams were sweet. No, she wasn't at all frightened of the beast anymore, they informed the ruler. She could even place her hand in its fire.

Her father decided to have her tailed.

The spy reported back that his daughter and the beast had picnicked together by the trout stream at the foot of the chase beyond the chestnut drive, on a salad of radishes, tomatoes and baby carrots they had picked themselves on the way.

'I don't want to hear the menu!' roared the ruler.

'The subjects then went swimming together,' the spy stumbled on. 'The young woman took off her dress and frolicked in the water until the salamander joined her.'

'Frolicked?' roared the ruler, again, lunging for the spy's throat.

'She wasn't naked,' he spluttered. 'She kept her petticoat on.'

'Petticoat?' The ruler threw the spy onto the floor and kicked him in the groin.

Then he gave the order for the arrest of the salamander.

That evening he summoned the palace spokesman and issued a statement.

'Since the unforeseeable arrival of the monstrous salamander on our shores, the number of catastrophes that have befallen our beloved people has increased apace. In view of this distressing and intolerable chain of events, and in reparation to the dead and the many victims afflicted in divers ways, it is hereby decided to bring the culprit to book. No longer shall we in our benevolence point to the hand of Fate: the mercy which we have shown before has been exhausted by the foul malice of the beast who has come among us. The monster is hereby charged with sedition against our state, for which the only penalty is death.'

In private, the ruler told the Press that he repented of his earlier scepticism. His daughter had been right to fear the creature; she – and the many God-fearing subjects in his kingdom – had shown greater wisdom than their loving ruler when they discerned divine judgement in the tragic events that had overtaken them. He begged forgiveness for his error, which rose from his desire not to see evil in others, but only good. Now, he realised, the devil was at work in his beloved country, and the salamander was his servant. With the extermination of the beast, their woes would cease.

'He was a malignant omen,' said the ruler to his weeping daughter. 'You were quite right, my dear. Since he appeared, there's been nothing but trouble.'

'Half the things happened before ever he . . .' But Estella faltered, when she saw the rage in her father's face. 'You know that,' she went on, under her breath.

She sat in court to hear the trial. Without the caresses of the beast's tongue on her flesh, she could not talk to him, nor he to her. Language between them had been altogether private, had enclosed their world and made it for each other alone. She stopped crying when she realised how bereft she was; all that was left inside her felt like a shaft of ice, frozen solid.

The trial was over rather quickly, given the silence of the defendant and the terror of the defence counsel who had been appointed to observe due process of law. The salamander was sentenced to be burned to death for the murder of thirty-five persons in the bullion vaults, the destruction of the library, the crash of the airbus, and the plague of Asiatic witchweed.

Estella, on the day of his death, took a handful of apricots in a scarf of shot green silk he had liked her to wear, a toothbrush and a change of underwear, and left the palace.

One of her maids heard her, but was loyal and did not give the alarm. When Estella reached the boundary fence she crawled under it, at the place that she and the salamander had dug together and kept concealed with brushwood. On the other side she stood a moment and spat on the ground, a curse on her father, and a curse on herself, too, for not running away with the salamander long before, when they were still safe in their secret.

The salamander was bound at the stake, like all traitors; but he did not burn. He lashed out, flames leaping from his jaws, until the exasperated ruler gave the order for the executioner to spear him through the heart. When the flames had died down, the beast was flayed and the flashing green trophy of his scaly skin displayed on a post in the main square. The faithful gazed on it in awe, and many sighed and gave thanks that the devil's henchman had been stopped in his evildoing. They applauded the ruler who, in his ineffable wisdom, had identified the author of their problem and rooted him out.

Long afterwards, when the ruler had been deposed, the government of the invaders bequeathed the salamander skin to the new Museum of Atrocities they had inaugurated. It was prominently displayed, next to a charred book, a witness, the label said, to the bygone ruler's attempt on History. The skin was still sulphorously green, and a pearly light played along the edges of the scales as vivid as in the creature's lifetime. Estella was in her early forties when she returned home – under a different name. She went to visit the mortal remnants of her dear friend once or twice, though she didn't need to look on his hide to remember their love. She didn't mourn; she knew he hadn't been the sort to want her to dwell on the past.

Dinosaur Dreams

DYAN SHELDON

Dyan Sheldon was born in the USA and now lives in London. She is the author of two novels, *Victim of Love* which was published by Heinemann in 1982 and by Penguin in 1984, and *Dreams of an Average Man* which was published by Heinemann in 1985 and by Penguin in 1986. Her short stories have been included in various anthologies, such as *Firebird, London Tales*, and *Winter Crimes*.

DINOSAUR DREAMS

Ann opens the door to the bathroom and looks in, her eyes wide and appraising, her smile as bright as the white ceramic tiles. 'This is very nice,' she says, approving of the stall shower and the heavy towels. 'Look, Richard, don't you think this is nice?'

But Richard, his back to her, is just shutting the door of the tiny refrigerator, into which he has deposited two bottles of wine, his face towards the main room: the colour television, the dark blue drapes, the subdued lighting, the thick carpet and solid sofa in matching, neutral tones, the adjustable table and the jug of water, the desk bedecked with flowers and cards, the Maypole of plastic tubes, the thin, still figure on the bed.

'First rate,' Richard says to his father. 'Don't you think?'

Richard's father, Roger, in his dark blue suit and polished brown shoes, sits on the sofa in front of the closed curtains, on his lap his opened briefcase, on the seat beside him the day's newspaper, on the small table to his left an empty cup of tea and a small plate dusted with crumbs. He almost looks like a commuter, waiting for his train. 'Excellent', he says, having looked up once, when they

130

first came in, and now not looking up again. 'I must say I'm very impressed.'

Richard moves the paper and sits beside him. 'I told you this hospital came highly recommended.' His eyes go to the images flickering across the television screen. Like their voices, the sound is turned down. 'It's nice to know she's in good hands,' he says.

Roger finishes the sentence he was writing, slips the lid back on his pen, closes the case, and puts it down on the floor. 'You get what you pay for,' he says. 'You can never go wrong when you pay for the best.'

Richard picks up the paper and glances at the headlines, more bad news, then turns to the day's listings.

Ann stands at the foot of the bed, smoothing out the already smooth blanket. 'So how is she?' she asks brightly. 'What do the doctors say?'

'The specialist says she has at least a sixty-forty chance of coming out of this better than new,' says Roger. He presses a button and changes the channel. 'He's the top man in his field – the experts' expert they call him – so I think he should know.'

'Sixty-forty,' says Richard. 'That's not bad at all.'

Roger's watch goes off, a sound as discreet and gentle as a butler's cough. He stills it with a touch. 'Of course there's no real way of knowing just yet. Until she's come round properly.' He looks at Ann, who is young and healthy and pretty and touching up her lipstick from a jet-black tube. 'It could be even better,' he tells her, just as the consultant told him. 'It all really depends on her.' He presses another button and changes the channel again. 'You know.'

Richard turns the page. 'They do amazing things nowadays,' he said, his attention caught by an article on holiday homes in Spain. 'Absolutely amazing. Twenty years ago, this sort of thing, but now . . . Miracles, really . . . not that mother needs a miracle of course. . . .'

Ann picks up the water pitcher, looks inside, then puts it back down. 'Will she be waking up soon, then?' she asks. 'She's not in a coma or anything is she?'

'Of course she's not in a coma,' says her father-in-law. 'She's sleeping.' He shifts his position, straightens the crease in his left trouser leg. 'She's had a lot of medication, of course.' He glances down at his briefcase. 'It could be a while.'

'Of course,' says Richard. 'Everybody's different. It could take hours.'

Roger returns the set to the original channel. 'I told her that as soon as she's up to it I'll take her to Paris for dinner,' he announces.

'Oh, how lovely,' says Ann. 'Does it have some special memory?'

Roger looks slightly surprised. 'Oh, no, no, no special memory. I just thought she'd like it.'

Ann smiles with understanding. 'How romantic,' she says. 'I suppose she's always wanted to go there.'

Roger smiles back, but unlike his daughter-in-law he looks confused. 'No, no, I don't think so. It just seemed like the place to go for something like that.' He picks a piece of fluff from his jacket. 'As you say, romantic.'

Thinking of Andalusia, where twenty years ago he spent two weeks with a crazy American girl who was doing Europe on a Triumph motorcycle, Richard looks up from the paper and says, 'How about a little wine?'

It is a warm room, quiet and tasteful, expensive but not ostentatious, modern but not flashy, the furnishings dark, the walls the colour of just-done toast. The reading lamps are on, violins play softly on the stereo, the sound so good you'd think they were in the room, a fire burns brightly in the grate. A perfect room, a room to envy. If it were in a painting you might want to climb in.

Outside the large bay window, whose curtains have not yet been drawn, the sky is mauve and streaked with gold, and blotched by near-black clouds. Roger looks up from his paper. He sees the shadows dancing around the flames like Indians, he sees the sunset and the changing light that makes the distant hills look yellow and blue, he sees his wife, her eyes wide and her expression rapt as she reads her magazine. He says, 'Fancy going out for dinner, dear? Feeling up to it tonight?'

Alice does not look up. 'You won't believe this, Roger,' she says, an unusual excitement in her voice. 'This is the most amazing thing I've ever heard of.'

'We could go to that new French place, down near the river,' says Roger. 'Richard says it's meant to be excellent, better than any place he's ever been to in France. Apparently the veal is out of this world.'

'Listen to this, Roger,' she says, as though she hasn't even heard him, 'just listen for a minute.'

His stomach rumbles. She's been a bit distracted since she came out of the hospital. He checks the time by the clock on the mantelpiece and wonders if he should have fried camembert as a starter, what the wine list is like. 'I just think that if we are going we'd better ring now,' he explains patiently. 'Richard says it gets quite crowded after eight.'

It is not like her not to agree with him. The success of their life together, he believes, is down to the fact that she has always followed his lead, shared his values, reflected his tastes, echoed his enthusiasms. To the fact that she always falls in with his plans.

But she is already reading in her thin, clear voice, still

strong, though since the operation she herself is pale and frail, some ridiculous story about dinosaurs in the Amazon. Stone-Age natives claiming to have seen them, to have taken them for granted for centuries, small, iridescent mountains moving in the distance, moving, like they themselves, slowly but determinedly through time. Dinosaur tracks being discovered by white men. Fresh tracks, not fossils. Footprints as big as a child. Not only that, but footprints less than a foot long as well. Baby dinosaurs.

She smiles at him across the coffee table, a tiny tinge of colour in her cheeks. 'Isn't that wonderful, Roger, baby dinosaurs? You never think of them having little ones, do you?'

'What I think, dear,' says Roger, forcing himself, after decades of speaking for the both of them, to choose his words carefully, 'is that you should probably take that article with a pinch of salt.' He smiles gently. He is a reasonable man. The doctors have warned him not to upset her, and upset her he won't. 'I mean, really, Alice, dinosaurs in this day and age?'

'Of course they wouldn't have discovered them till now,' says Alice, sounding as logical as ever she was. 'It's only now that they'd started chopping the forest down. It was impenetrable before.' Her glasses have slid down her nose and she peers over them at him, just like always, as though she is making a point about the garden or the neighbours or the parish fête, as though she is about to agree with him on what sort of new car to buy, where to go for their winter holiday.

He notices that she is holding the magazine so that he can't see the page she's been reading. He is not going to say anything about her medication, about painkillers, about her months on drugs. 'So how do you feel?' he asks. 'Shall we go out?'

'So,' Roger is saying, 'did you take my advice about that investment?'

Richard opens the second bottle with a pop. 'And bloody glad I am, too,' he grins. 'I told Ann, "if my father says it's a certainty, then a certainty it is." ' He fills their glasses, real glasses, not paper cups, not tooth mugs. It is not only his father who is capable of giving good advice. 'At least when the time comes to start a family,' he says, not meeting Ann's eyes, 'at least we'll know we can send them to decent schools.'

Roger chuckles. 'You'll be able to educate an army on what that stock's going to bring in in the next ten years.'

'I'm not as adventurous as you are, Dad,' says Richard, who isn't, who when he was small wanted to be a librarian or a fisherman, ambitions that made his father laugh and take him into the office with him and sit him at his desk. 'I like to know I have something aside for a rainy day.' He turns so that his back is to the bed. 'You never know what's going to happen.'

Roger brushes away doubt with one hand. 'Happen? What's going to happen? You're both young. You've got at least another thirty years before you have to worry about anything happening. And by then . . .' he shrugs. 'By then who knows? We've got the world in our pockets for the first time in history.' He pulls a corner of the drapes aside and looks out at the city below them, its lights bright and steady, stretching out to the edges of darkness and beyond. To Richard he says, 'It's what I've always said to your mother,' but it is to Ann that he turns. 'Alice is not a silly woman,' he says, making it clear that he thinks she and Ann are the exceptions, 'but even she has the occasional romantic notion.' He smiles, one hand still holding the edge of the curtain aside. 'Every time there's another hijacking or someone goes crazy and guns down a playground full of children, she gets sentimental about the past. You know, thinks she'd like to live in the eighteenth century or some such rubbish, thinks things were better then, slower,' taking one last glance out the window, 'more gentle. But she's only kidding herself, I tell her. This is the best time to be alive there's ever been.' The curtain falls back in place. 'We've got everything. We're prosperous, stable, we've just about wiped out poverty – '

'Well, Dad,' jokes Richard, emboldened by the *blanc de blanc*, 'there is the Third World.'

'We are not in the Third World, Richard,' his father points out.

'Thank God,' says Ann, who has still not forgiven Richard for suggesting Mexico for their honeymoon. 'What, and die in an earthquake?' she had wanted to know. 'We'll go to the Bahamas, like everybody else.'

'We've got everything going for us. When has it ever been better? I'm not saying we don't have any problems, but just look around you. We're just at the point where we control the world rather than the other way around . . .' he gestures with his glass towards his wife, his cufflinks twinkling. 'Just look at your mother,' he says. 'Medicine. Look at all that medicine can do. Transplants, test-tube babies, you name it . . . We live longer and better, soon we won't even get old – '

'Oh, I know, Dad,' says Richard quickly, 'I only meant – '

'Alice?' says Ann, suddenly getting to her feet and going over to the side of the bed. 'Alice?' But there is no change in position, no movement of an eyelid, no sound but the shallowest of breathing.

'What is it, honey?' asks Richard, finishing off the wine in his glass. 'Is she awake?'

'I thought she said something.'

'She's just dreaming,' says Roger. 'It's the drugs.'

'I hope we get there soon,' says Roger, fiddling with the radio, trying to retrieve the news. 'I could eat a dinosaur,' he grins.

Once, when Richard was very young, she wanted to float kites over the garden for his birthday. Dragons and fish and diamonds and stars. It had come to her in a dream, a vision of the garden, glowing in the summer sunshine, and above it a dozen kites, bright as flowers, waving at the sky, but Roger had said it was an impractical idea, that it would take hours to get the kites up, that there might not be any wind, that they would be expensive, that the children wouldn't appreciate it, a clown and a pony and a cake made to look like a train would give them a lot more pleasure, that the kites would only end up drifting away or gathering dust in the loft. She'd known, of course, that he was right, but at this moment, as she gazes out the window, her face against the breeze, thinking about the dinosaurs, the dinosaurs plodding quietly through the jungle for all those millions of years and now having no place to go, she can almost see those kites, flickering like stars, and wonders if he hadn't been wrong.

Somehow, he has taken a wrong turning. The road has become narrow and rutted, the houses and lights, water tanks and smokestacks, aerials and electricity poles and satellite dishes have all disappeared. 'This isn't the road to the river,' says Roger, picking up speed. The evening is not so much darkening as thickening, growing jungle-like around them, as though they're standing still.

There is a fragrance in the air that seems familiar, forgotten but familiar, some aroma as intoxicating as that very first glass of wine. 'Of course it is,' says Alice, so drunk, it seems, that she sounds certain. 'What's that shining down there through those trees if it isn't the river?'

'What, dear?' says Roger, not losing his temper, as once he might have done. 'I can't hear you when you talk into the wind.'

She turns her head. 'Down there,' she says, her voice softer, pointing, 'isn't that the river?'

The car bounces. 'My God,' says Roger, 'what's happened to the paving? We seem to be on a dirt track.'

Alice leans her head into the night, where something calls. 'Can you hear that?' she asks. 'Isn't it beautiful? It must be a bird.'

'Did you hear me?' asks Roger, loudly in order to catch her attention. 'I said we've left the road.'

'Though, I must say, it isn't any bird I've ever heard before.' She puts one hand to her head to hold on her hat as the car bucks and pitches over the rocks and ruts. 'I used to be very good on birds.'

'What?' They are no longer on a dirt track, they are on a path, a path made without the dimensions of a Mercedes in mind. Branches scrape against the silver-grey body and snap beneath the white-walled wheels. 'What did you say, Alice? Did you say you could see the river?'

The glass doors open automatically.

'What a terrific neighbourhood,' says Ann, as she steps into the lobby with its carpet and couches and plants and tiny shops and visitors reading paperbacks and magazines. 'I wouldn't mind living around here myself. What do you think Richard? We passed some beautiful houses. Did you notice?'

'I'd move here just to be near that restaurant,' says Richard. 'That was the best Thai food I've ever had.' He shakes his head in wonder. 'Can you imagine? So far from the centre of town.'

'One of the things I like most about this place,' says Roger, 'is that you'd hardly know you were in a hospital at all.'

'Absolutely,' agrees Ann, as they enter the lift. 'Can you imagine how depressing it must be to be in one of those awful grim places where people. . . .' She was about to say 'are dying', but her husband and her father-in-law, happy with the excellent meal and relaxed after their amiable talk of business ventures and the world situation and the condominium they might buy together in Miami and the play they will all see when Alice is recovered, are smiling at her so warmly that instead she finishes with '. . . well, you know what I mean, it must be just dreadful.'

The room is just as they left it, except that the pitcher has been refilled and the light nearest the bed has been dimmed.

'She's still sleeping,' says Richard, pouring himself a glass of water. 'How much longer do they think she'll be out?'

Roger hangs up his coat and jacket in the closet. 'The doctor on duty's not the specialist, of course, but he thought she'd wake up soon.' He shuts the door soundlessly. 'I think we should stay as long as we can. We wouldn't want her coming round and thinking she was all alone.'

'She looks so peaceful,' says Ann, standing at the foot of the bed. 'Almost as though she's smiling.'

Roger settles himself on the sofa. 'She's getting the best care in the world. She's got her family nearby. And in time the only thing she'll remember about the whole experience is going home.' The locks on his briefcase snap open. 'Why shouldn't she be smiling?' he wants to know.

The night comes down suddenly and completely, as though someone pushed a button, at about the same time that the car comes to an abrupt halt, up to its bumper in some sort of sludge, thick shrubs pressed around it like curtains.

'What the hell . . .' says Roger, putting it into reverse, trying to rock them free. 'What is this stuff?' The car sinks deeper. He turns on the lights, both inside and out. Forgetting her close call and her weakened condition, he turns on his wife. 'I thought you said this was the way to the river,' he shouts. 'I thought you said you knew where we were going.'

But Alice is already undoing her seatbelt. 'Just look at those flowers,' she says, her face flushed, her eyes star-bright, her voice almost girlish with excitement. 'Jut listen to those birds. Just smell the air.'

'Flowers? Birds? Air?' His waving hand accidentally turns on the wipers. 'Since when are you so interested in nature, Alice?'

She gives him a look he doesn't really understand, and certainly doesn't remember ever having seen before.

In his haste to turn off the wipers, he hits the horn. 'I know you like the garden, you're very good with the gar – '

She turns her eyes away from him. 'And see,' she says, her tone nearly normal, pointing through the windscreen as though there is something out there besides trees, 'there's the river, right down there.'

Roger refuses to get out of the car. He leaves the engine running, leaves the lights on, and, giving up on the radio, puts a cassette into the player, Wagner. 'I just don't know what's got into you, Alice,' he says. 'It's madness getting out of this car. Sheer madness.'

'And what do you suggest we do?' asks Alice crisply. 'Sit here all night? Just sit here in this car?'

'And what's wrong with that?' Roger hangs up the phone, flips open the glove compartment and removes a silver flask. 'It's warm. It's dry. It's safe. The seats go back and there's a blanket in the boot. As soon as Richard gets home he'll get my message on the machine and arrange to have us picked up.'

She has always listened to him, Alice, has always taken his advice on everything from dressing for dinner to making love – but she isn't listening to him now. She is putting on the old, flat shoes she keeps in the car for driving, a hard look in her eyes.

'You're crazy, Alice. You've been ill. What would the doctor say? You're in no condition to go gallivanting in the wild. Why can't you just stay put? You won't go a yard in that mud.'

She opens the door, letting in the damp, spiky night with all its dark, furtive sounds, its rustlings and hummings and crackings and something lonesome wailing just beyond the trees.

'You'll sink like a rock, Alice. Mark my words.'

She steps out, unsinking, smiling in the lunar light.

'You'll get stuck, Alice.' He takes a shot of whisky, warmer than a kiss. 'And don't think I'm going to rescue you, either. This is one time you can't count on me.'

She slams the door behind her. 'I'm going down to the river,' she says calmly, cheerfully, as though they aren't parked in a swamp in the middle of nowhere, bats swooping across the bonnet, the woods moaning, the stars sharp as knives. 'That's why we've come here and that's where I'm going.'

'We came to eat a decent meal in a decent restaurant, not tramp around in the muck,' shouts Roger. 'Listen, Alice, listen to those sounds. There's no telling what's out there, Alice. Waiting. Waiting for you.'

She stops a few feet away, turning towards him but not bending down so she can see him clearly. She has always done what he said. She has always wanted to. Call it love or call it something else, she has always wanted to do what he said. But not tonight. Tonight the stars hang in the sky like kites and in what remains of the jungle the dinosaurs roam.

'Well,' says Alice, 'there's only one way to find out.'

He pushes a button and the windows roll up. He pushes another button and the door locks click closed. He takes another drink.

Alice is already deep in the dark.

Away from the car, the trees are not so dense, the ground is firm, the moon so bright she barely hesitates or stumbles or worries as she makes her way down to the river. She hasn't been out at night in decades – only to go from a building to a car or a car to a building, only to check that the lawn chairs had been brought in or the garage light was on. She picks a large, purple flower, never grown in any garden, and sticks it jauntily into the band of her hat. Alice doesn't feel afraid. Alice doesn't feel ill. Alice doesn't feel tired, or bored, or old, or, she realises, any of the other things she has been feeling for such a long long time. Any of the things she's become. She marches on, nearly dizzy with delight, right left right left, sliding down a slight incline, climbing up the other side. There below is the river. What does she feel? She sits down at the top of the hill, right on the ground in her good brown suit. She feels like a child. She feels like a child, a lifetime ahead and everything exciting, everything interesting, everything new. She feels that there is something waiting for her out there, something wonderful, for her alone. Just like a child.

A star falls. Something lost and longing and lonesome cries, and Alice turns to look. There, just coming around the bend, is a herd of dinosaurs, shining in the moonlight, the largest as big as the hill on which she sits, the smallest no bigger than a pony. Alice moves closer to the edge of the rise. Three large dinosaurs, pink and purple and new-grass green; three baby dinosaurs, ocean blue. The babies waddle on their stubby little legs, bumping heads, nuzzling, leaning one against the other, yipping playfully – but the adults walk slowly and determinedly, like wanderers, like refugees, drawn without will, their eyes towards the heavens, their voices mournful, sounding at the end of a long, sad song. And yet rather than sadness they fill her with joy. The dinosaurs, she thinks, her heart racing, the dinosaurs are real. Real after all. Still survive. Alice, lying on her stomach, watches them move up the riverbank as the moon moves across the sky.

Richard and Ann doze on the sofa, blankets thrown across them, their breathing as sure and regular as the ticking of a clock. Roger sits in the chair at the bedside, a pillow wedged under his head, thinking about the house and the office, his secretary's upcoming holiday and the housekeeper's refusal to come in an extra day, wondering what he's done with the ticket from the dry cleaners and if the boy next door remembered to feed the dog.

The night is long. Footsteps softly pass along the corridor, voices can be heard talking loudly on the street, whispering or moaning or, once, calling out from other rooms. Now and then a buzzer sounds or a fragment of song drifts in or, outside where the stars are barely visible, a siren howls.

When she wakes up, the dinosaurs are still there.

Colony of Despots

GEORGINA ANDREWES

Georgina Andrewes was born in 1959 in Winch-
ester, Hampshire. She read Natural Sciences and
took a postgraduate Certificate of Education at
Cambridge University and then worked for two
years with VSO in Kenya, teaching science and
maths in a community school. She now works
as a presenter for the African service of the BBC.
Her first novel, *Behind the Waterfall*, was published by Pandora Press in 1988 and won the
Betty Trask Award.

COLONY OF DESPOTS

On the sand on the shore of a faraway island the Ruler sat and stared at the sea. It was over forty years since the invaders had ousted him from his great seat of power and banished him from the land he'd controlled with such might. He was now a very old man, how old he couldn't be sure; his eyesight was weak, his hands crippled in unnatural contortions and he no longer had the control of his bladder that was proper for such a man of importance. He worried about this: that he would be taken short when they invited him home for the magnificent unveiling of his statue outside the Palace of Parliament.

The sun was rising, the sea still an early morning silver, not yet the brilliant interminable blue that surrounded the tiny atoll and stretched before him day after day. Every morning he would sit here and chant history until the sun was over the palm trees and the sand had begun to shimmer.

'Dum-de-dum-de-dum, eighty-one, power begun,
Doo-de-doo-de-doo, eighty-two, attempted coup,
Executions, quite a few.'

History, of course, should be written down, but the

scholars and biographers had been busy with that. Here on the island with no pens or paper he could merely keep it alive in memory, lest the historians should omit any detail or distort any fact. It was remarkable how sharp his mind remained, something lesser men had always admired, his striking ability to grasp the essence of an issue in the flash of a razorshell. He reached the end of the morning's incantation and poked a piece of driftwood at a nearby crab. A giant green-carapaced creature whose meat was sweet to eat, it scuttled for cover of a rock and crouched there waving back a threatening claw. But the Ruler had lost interest, his crabbing days were over, he survived on seaweed and tins of beans and spaghetti rings from the box of groceries that came each month. They never let him go without food, no more, no less, every month the box of provisions carefully packed, tins on the bottom, boxes of biscuits on top, wedged together with scrumpled newspaper. These days the subtle flavours of lobster, crab and stewed anemones would be lost to his scummy palate. And after all, hadn't he taken a strong ecological stand in his later years of office?

The Ruler stood up and taking the driftwood for a stick he slowly made his way to the water's edge. He was wearing a sea-stained pair of long white shorts, and looked, as old men do when naked, loose-skinned and frail. A shoal of silver fish slipped between his toes as he waded into the shallows and bent to scoop some water in an old plastic cup. He poured it over his head, spitting and slobbering as it trickled through his yellowed hair and over his sun-blotched face.

Back in his small house in the clearing in the palm trees he put on a suit and tie. It took longer these days to wash and dress, his lock-jointed fingers grappled with the buttons of his shirt as if sheathed in heavy gloves. But he must look smart, they would expect him to look the part when they delivered the first of the great volumes.

The guard hovered behind him, as he had hovered on the beach, as these athletic uniformed men with their tin hats and polished guns shadowed him wherever he went. A testimony to his power, but they even stood guard as he slept, witnesses to his snoring and farting; he'd heard them laughing as they went off duty. Such intrusion was criminal. He eased himself into the broken wicker chair on the balcony and smoothed out a sheet of newspaper that he'd salvaged from the most recent load of groceries. The sports page; he'd never cared for sport, the pursuit of lazy men who didn't want to work, unwelcome immigrants, though useful on occasion for the national image. The guard brought his breakfast: a single piece of toast and marmalade and a strong pot of tea. He didn't thank him, it had been his policy not to speak to anyone but himself. He took out a pair of spectacles, the gold-rimmed, half-moon ones he'd worn on execution days, he put them on and hid behind the racing results so the guard wouldn't see the dribble on his chin as he chewed the toast. Today, it must be today, the great encyclopaedias of history would arrive. He savoured the thought, and felt the sweat rise on his brow with the tremor of expectation. They'd be leather-bound, of course, perhaps a dark red leather, gold-embossed. How many would there be? He couldn't imagine less than twenty.

A lizard, lime-green and scaly-skinned, shot down the wall and strutted mechanically across the verandah to settle in a patch of sun. Revolting, prehistoric creature. The guard took away the breakfast tray, another guard came on duty. Flies buzzed irritatingly past the protruding white hairs of the old man's nose and settled around a blob of marmalade on his tie. He grunted, snorted and his head lolled forward onto his chest. The Ruler slept.

When he woke, well over two hours later, there was a great commotion down on the shore, guards shouting and waving at each other and those off duty running from their huts in only their trousers. The old man heaved himself from his chair and went down the steps from the balcony to take a better look. A sleek white yacht was motoring into the bay. Excitement welled up within him, a glorious surge that he hadn't felt in years. It used to come as he prepared to address the crowds, as they played the national anthem and the cameras swung in on him, stern, ruthless. Marvellous. A slight dampening of his trousers. Composure – he must remain composed, calm, proud, worthy of all that was written of him, the great Ruler of decades gone by. The boat came to anchor a short way offshore, he watched the guards wading out, with their uniforms rolled above their knees. A large trunk was lowered overboard; it took five men to steady it and like a coffin they bore it high on their shoulders as they carried it to land. Gratitude was an emotion he didn't see fit to express – this was his due – but his first thought was not far from thanks, a glimmer of grateful pleasure, that they'd taken the trouble to pack the books in a sturdy sea-worthy trunk that would withstand the damp and crustiness of the sea.

Golden Butterfly, the First Lady, refused to come above deck.

'I'm a lady, I'm a queen,' she whined, 'you can't imprison me!'

She was dressed as royalty, in a long gown of turquoise satin, the sleeves puffed, the neckline scooped above her bosom and the bodice embroidered with tiny silken flowers. Her black hair was piled high, lacquered and shining, a diamond tiara sparkling in its midst. The young guards, undeterred, moved in on her.

'Tie her hands!' one of them shouted.

'You grab her feet!'

The gold stiletto sandals slipped from her heels as she was passed horizontally out of the cabin.

'Ruffians! The indignity!' she squealed, as the muscular men handed her overboard to their waiting comrades.

'Rats! Vermin! Take me home. Don't you know who I am?'

They carried her, like the chest, high above their heads and laid her beside it on the sand. A pale-faced guard undid the ties about her wrists.

'Take your filthy hands off me! You ugly little worm!'

The young man clenched his jaw and released her plump brown arms. The First Lady struggled to stand up, the dress, already taut along the bulging seams, allowed little room for movement. She pulled herself onto the chest and glared at the guards. Dark eyes, heavy-lidded, cheeks unnaturally taut for a woman of her age, the skin stretched back towards her ears, pinned and tucked and caked with makeup. She delicately brushed the sand from the satin and adjusted her tiara.

'How filthy it is! I can't possibly live here.' The jowly folds of her neck, creased and criss-crossed with tiny lines, trembled as she spoke.

At home in her heyday, she'd imported hundreds of tons of pure white sand for her private beach. It had given her exquisite pleasure to scoop it in her palm and let it trickle between her long brown fingers in a fine flow of tiny grains. 'Your skin is as smooth as the purest sand,' her admirers had told her and she'd cooed and smiled.

150

Here the sand was grey and strewn with rotting weed and the dismembered carcasses of foul-smelling crabs.

One of the soldiers poked her with his rifle butt. 'Stand up. Move!'

The First Lady gathered up her dress about her ankles.

'My shoes,' she sobbed, 'my pearls! Thieves!'

The Ruler took the inland path through the scrub and dense vegetation so that he wouldn't be seen approaching the bay. He noted with disgust that the Emperor had already been out; his traps were newly-sprung with fresh bloody meat and sharpened razor blades. There was a line of unwanted small mammals, headless and tail-less, laid across the track. Further on, lay the skulls of former cruelties, daubed with melted tar that had washed up on the beach and stuck with the red and green feathers of parrots. The Ruler swiped at them with his stick. The black barbarian should have been executed years ago. He would have had him flogged and hanged.

The Emperor, a squat, bull-faced man, crouched in his hide amidst the blade-tussocked dunes. He pulled on a nostril and scratched between his legs. Sweat was soaking through his military uniform and pouring down his face. He'd used his handkerchief to tie up the morning's collection of livers and kidneys for lunch. He wiped a hand across his forehead and twiddled the tight-curled hairs of his beard – it gave him a pleasantly sensual sensation, which heightened his expectation. The trunk looked just about big enough to hold a tender-fleshed slave girl shipped from the mainland. Black or white it didn't matter, he'd been so long without a vessel for his manliness. He would enjoy her company tonight; first impress her with his medals and hunting trophies, the diamond-studded elephant tusks and fearsome head of the man-

151

eating lion, then spread his coronation cloak upon the floor, open a bottle of Napoleon brandy and eat his favourite island delicacy of monkeys' brains wrapped in vine leaves from her naked buttocks. He fanned his face with an old giraffe tail whisk. Hunting couldn't satisfy all his natural urges.

The Ruler had taken up watch behind a palm tree. He noted a guard standing by the hide on the edge of the dunes and knew the dark-skinned Emperor was in residence – spying as usual. Mosquitoes whined about the old man's ears; he twitched away from them like a solitary horse pestered by flies, then felt one settle and sink through the thin skin of his neck. Bloodthirsty creature. They said the black man used to eat the bodies of his enemies, stuffed with rice and flamed in gin. Did gin flame? He wasn't sure, brandy perhaps. Occasionally he had nightmares of burning corpses, uncertain when he woke whether it was he or the Emperor who presided over the furnace.

For twenty years the Ruler and the Emperor had scorned each other's company, meeting only for their annual health checks at the Commandant's office. The humiliating procedure of removing their clothes in the same room had reinforced their mutual disgust; the Emperor smelt of dead monkeys, the Ruler of the worst French lavatories. This year the Commandant, a solid, dummy-faced man, had announced that another prisoner was soon to join them.

'Any requests?' he snapped. The two old men, now dressed again, stood side by side in front of his desk. A grey-finned fan clicked round above their heads circulating the sweat-stale air. 'According to the terms of your imprisonment you may ask for something to be delivered with the third and final prisoner.' His pen was poised

above a blue printed paper. 'There'll be no more consider-
ations after this.'

The Emperor puffed himself up and let out a noise not
far from a chuckle. 'A woman, *s'il vous plaît.*'

The Commandant looked down, wrote, looked up
again.

'Sir,' the Ruler began. He was not in the habit of speaking. 'As you know,' his voice sounded weak, he was
acutely aware of the movement of his jaw, 'I held a position of great importance for very many years. I am most
anxious to read the history books.' He fumbled in his
pocket for the piece of newspaper that he'd rescued from
the grocery box. 'I happened to come across a small advertisement for "*The History of the Modern World* – A DEFINI-
TIVE SET OF ENCYCLOPAEDIAS BY LEADING
HISTORIANS – FREE ON APPROVAL FOR
TWENTY-ONE DAYS." '

On the shore the fat blue woman was clinging to the
trunk. A couple of guards pulled her away and prodded
her along the beach. The others remained surrounding
the padlocked chest.

'My shoes!' she cried.

The Ruler watched her picking her way through the
debris of the beach, her stout torso thrust forward stiffly
as she took dainty steps of self-conscious dignity. More
Third World riff-raff. Another plunderer of national cof-
fers, dripping with ridiculous jewels. Why did they bring
them here, when he was such a civilised man? He turned
back along the bush path, confident at least that the books
were in the safekeeping of the guards. He was a patient
man, he could wait to be summoned for the official pres-
entation.

'The Emperor smiled and stroked his thighs as the

woman passed within yards of his cover. Nice broad bottom.

'Give me my shoes!' she hissed at the guards.

Once, the First Lady had owned over three thousand pairs of shoes.

'A lie, of course,' she told the Emperor. They were sitting now on the balcony of her house sipping lime juice from the prison beakers. The sun was glowing red and sinking towards the sea. 'A malicious lie. Trying to discredit me in front of my people. I only ever had a thousand and sixty. I made them count them.'

'Italian?'

'Of course, and French – I adore Paris.'

The Emperor glowed with approval. He'd had many rich years in France.

'We were the greatest friends, the President and I.' He stroked his beard.

'Of course, how wonderful!'

The Emperor cleared his throat and spat on the floor. 'He appreciated the diamonds I gave him.'

The First Lady held up the metal beaker and swivelled it round trying to catch a glimpse of her face – but the image which should have been so perfect was infuriatingly dull and distorted.

'I lo – ve diamonds,' she sighed. 'So,' she searched for a word, 'so pretty.'

They were sitting in wicker chairs a few feet apart, their soft flesh pressing into the ungiving cane. The Emperor leant forward, the medals swinging from his chest, and placed a hand on her knee, just high enough to feel the fat of her thigh. He moistened his lips with his thick pink tongue.

'I welcome your sophisticated company,' he said.

A mediocre, self-important man, she thought, a typical hanger-on. But she shivered at the prospect of diamonds. Her eyelids fluttered, her lips parted.

'I can tell you're a kind man,' she pouted a little. 'Everybody's been so cruel to me.'

The guards' feet made no sound as they trod the damp sand with the leather trunk roped to poles on their shoulders. But the rhythm of their movement pushed through the air as they neared the prisoners' houses. It was now dark. Moths dived and frizzled on the naked flame of a paraffin lamp; the Ruler studied their charred corpses, moments of flight singed to stillness, with a mean uncaring interest. His face was ugly in the shadowy half light of dusk: the mouth drawn tight, the eyes inhumanly still, like those of a man beating a little boy. He looked across to the First Lady's house a short way along the shore. There the balcony was strung with lamps that glowed like milky fat grubs. She was singing, the romantic trill carried through the calm air and assaulted his ears. Where were the guards? The frivolous little lady should be properly controlled. His State Police would have dealt nicely with her. More fear and less freedom – that was the essence of control. He smiled to himself, the thin-lipped mouth relaxing, the corners turning down in a quivering self-satisfied leer.

The trunk was heavy, it swayed this way and that with the uneven steps as the guards negotiated a torch-lit path through the squelching dark bodies of weed and angry scavenging crabs. Every hundred paces they lowered it to the ground, changed positions on the poles and took up the load again.

The Ruler thought of the books; he closed his eyes and saw the bold type on the cream-coloured pages, a full-page photograph, an opening chapter on his rapid rise to power, then the fear he'd engendered, the expulsion of immigrants, expansion of the army, control of the Press. Even the unfortunate loss of life would now be seen as necessary to the greater scheme of things. They could end with the victories of his third war, the crushing of the people's uprising, the reintroduction of capital punishment.

'Prisoners assemble on the sand!' The Commandant's voice came over the tannoy, echoing and disembodied.

There it was, they stood before it, the vast, battered leather trunk. There were a couple of old sticky labels on its side, indicating journeys made before from an English to a Spanish port, the hinges were rusted, the leather straps worn where the buckles had rubbed, but the padlock sturdy and shining new. The First Lady was sobbing with excitement, clasping her hands to her face. The Emperor stood to attention, straightening his jacket, smoothing it over his rounded stomach. The Ruler stared. For a moment his bones seemed to seize, his breath no longer draw, his heart began to slow. Then the old lust overwhelmed him: 'I', he thought, rolling the single ego-centric syllable round in his head, pushing it between his lips like a gust of cold wind, I, I, I am there in that chest. '*Immortal, Invisible,*' a long-forgotten hymn stirred within and rattled in his throat, '*God, only wise.*'

The Commandant dismissed the guards, he unlocked the padlock and pushed back the heavy lid.

The First Lady was out at dawn arranging her army of shoes along the balcony, counting as she lifted them from cocoons of tissue paper and pointed their toes to face the sea. She unpacked the last pair and returned along the row inspecting the stiletto heels. It was ten days since she'd arrived on the island, time to send another present to the Emperor; she carefully wrapped a pearl-studded slipper.

The Emperor was eating octopus for breakfast; his body suffused with sublime pleasure as the slimy tentacles, stewed in coconut milk, slid gently down his gullet. He picked up the dish and drank the last of the juice, wiped his mouth with his hand, then went inside to prise another diamond from the ivory elephant tusk. He'd wasted no time in responding to the First Lady's advances – nor she to his – and now, locked forever in ludicrous mutual admiration, they sent their gifts back and forth along the shore.

The Ruler remained alone. He had his books. He sat in the wicker chair with the leather-bound volumes stacked around him. He no longer slept or washed or bothered to eat. He no longer went down to the shore to chant. Day and night he studied the books. He pored over them, his back hunched in concentration as he turned the thick pages with their sharp smell of printers' ink. He'd expected a volume to himself, charting three glorious decades of power, but his name wasn't embossed in gold on a cover or a spine. So he'd taken each volume in turn, and scoured the chapters, flicking through the pages, his mouth dribbling, his eyes watering, searching for the section dedicated to him. The guard brought his meals, slices of corned beef that curled in the sun, spaghetti that congealed in the middle of the plate, then took them away again. Sometimes the old man fell asleep, then woke with a start, fearing that the guards were stealing the books. He fumbled for his stick and tapped the volumes; nineteen on the floor, one on his lap, a firm weight on his frail legs, pressing hard on his useless bladder. He pushed his spectacles over the bony white ridge of his nose and muttered to himself. Impossible, to write of the London Summit without mention of him, the nuclear arms talks, the war of '98. He thumped the page with his fist. How could they? Pain seared through his arthritic fingers. He thrust the book from his knees. He could hear the First Lady singing and monkeys screaming in the trees. A hateful breed, historians. He hauled another book from the floor and gripped it by the spine, his pulse pounding in the thin blue veins of his wrist.

The guards came and went on their daily shifts. Perhaps some pages had stuck together, or a volume was missing. He began again, reading slowly, every page of every volume, running a finger down the lines, finding nothing, his mind numbed by the scheming and warring of other men's lives. Strands of spit hung from his open mouth and fell on the pages, he blotted them with the sleeve of his jacket. His stomach churned, he swallowed hard, fighting down the hollow pain. A mistake, that's all, a wretched, careless mistake. He bent over the last book and thumbed the index, searching like a desperate man after gold, panning the words for his name, now just his name, just once, a single name, somewhere, amidst all these pages of history. But there was nothing, nothing at all.

The Foul Weather Friend

MAEVE BINCHY

Maeve Binchy was born in Dublin and went to school at the Holy Child Convent in Killiney. She took a history degree at UCD and taught in various girls' schools, writing travel articles in the long summer holidays. In 1969 she joined the *Irish Times*. For some ten years she has been based in London and writes humorous columns from all over the world.

The Peacock Theatre in Dublin was the scene of her two stage plays, *End of Term* and *Half Promised Land*; her television play, *Deeply Regretted by* won two Jacobs Awards and the Best Script prize at the Prague Film Festival.

She is the author of several volumes of short stories, among them *London Transports*, *Dublin 4* and *The Lilac Bus*. Her novels include *Light a Penny Candle*, *Echoes* (which was transmitted on Channel 4 in May 1988) and her most recent bestseller *Firefly Summer*. A new collection of interlinked short stories, *Silver Wedding*, was published in October 1988.

She is married to the writer and broadcaster Gordon Snell.

THE FOUL WEATHER FRIEND

Whenever I look at my telephone answering machine
winking at me as I come in, I think of my friend.
I bought the answering machine once because of a
friend.
A good friend indeed but a foul weather friend.

She stood by the bus stop the day that I met her first, so
thin, so frail that I thought a strong gust of wind coming
around that corner might brush her and make her hit her
head against the shelter. Her head seemed very large: a
lot of very frizzy brown hair, not an Afro cut, but as if
someone had gone around it shaving little bits off like
those pom-pom tassles we used to make at school. I
looked at her hair for a long time, not realising I was
staring. Probably a lot of people stand at that bus stop
not realising they are staring. It's just outside the hospital.
I wanted to think of anything except the face of my friend,
Maria, who wouldn't see me, who sat in her room (they
won't call it a cell), dealing and redealing those cards. Not
ordinary playing cards but Tarot cards with Swords and
Cups and Pentacles. Hour after hour she sits there, laying
them out in the shape of a cross and mumbling to them.

John didn't know I had been. He had begged me not to go. We made her this way, he had said so often. This is our punishment. I had tried to laugh him out of it. I am the Irish Catholic, I told him, if there is a sense of Sin I should have it. He was brought up in a house where nobody talked conversationally about Hell like we all did. Yet he was the one with the huge Guilt that ended our love. We had betrayed Maria, he her husband, I her best friend. I stood staring at the big fuzzy head of the pale woman who hugged her arms around her thin waist as if she were trying to hold the top half of her trunk in some unsatisfactory way to the rest of her body.

She spoke to me without smiling.

'My name is Fenella,' she said.

'I only read that kind of name in school stories.' It was true. Fenella was always the plucky one or the tomboy even. Nobody back home was called Fenella.

'You're very upset, aren't you?' she asked. She had so much compassion in her voice I could have reached out and touched her, helped her to hold that thin body together for fear of its breaking and one half being swept away. She hadn't made a Bus Stop remark about there never being any kind of transport when you needed it. She hadn't made a Hospital remark about having to be grateful for having your own health. She looked at me and saw my hurt and unhappiness; they were so clear for her to see that she had spoken of them.

I thought it was only the sharp, cold wind that stung my eyes as it whistled around the high walls of the hospital but it was her sympathy that made my eyes sting. No stranger had ever reached out, spoken to me like that before. Not even back home where they often spoke almost too directly and came too far into your life. But in England of all places. In the manicured, leafy lanes of the Home Counties outside the well-pointed walls of a private mental hospital. A complete stranger had said that she could see my upset. I felt like a fool as the tears rolled down. She put out her arm and I thought she was going to embrace me, so I flinched a little. But no, it was just that the bus was coming.

'It's a request stop,' she said gently. 'You have to ask it nicely, otherwise it will just pass by.' She was trying to make me smile, I think, to look less like someone who had escaped from behind those high walls.

She paid my fare on the bus and came into my life.

In the town she knew a place where they served home-made soup and lovely whole wheat rolls. It was comfort food, the tables were far apart. Nobody except Fenella heard my tale of John and Maria, and how it had all been her fault, how she had a perfectly happy life until she took off in hot pursuit of Carlos, how it had unhinged her. I told her of the lonely days and nights and how John and I had consoled each other in the only way great and good friends could do, by loving and giving. And how I had hoped she would find happiness with her Carlos and her mad quests. But John wanted things tidied up, he hated loose ends. and now they were tidy all right: John a workaholic who made Maria mad as birds in a place she would never leave and as for me. . . . It's odd but I never remember telling anyone as much as I told Fenella, not only that afternoon in the warm Soup Kitchen . . . with its crackling fire and its crusty rolls and its deep, warming, reviving, steaming bowls of good things, but later, that evening, on the train back to London, and that night when she said it didn't seem wise to leave me alone, and she came back to my flat. She sat in a chair and her hair was like a halo. I thought she was indeed some kind of saint, ready to listen, and listen. Always wanting to hear more. Never a word of blame. And what was so wonderful was that she never once tried to cheer me up. There was no point where she said I would get over him and find someone else. She never warned me that all men were some variety of louse and that time spent weeping over them was time wasted. She didn't offer me hope that Maria would die, that John would come to his senses and beg me to return to his side; she just accepted that things were utterly terrible and shared the burden with me.

Soon I felt a great great tiredness. I welcomed it like you'd welcome rain when it has been a close day. It had been so long since my shoulders and eyes had been tired. Normally I sat awake tense and smoking for most of the night. In the staff room at school I knew they must have noticed how short-tempered and irritable I had become. A wave of resentment towards them all came over me. These were my colleagues and indeed friends for nearly a decade. How had none of THEM spotted my grief and been able to listen, to understand, and to be such a great friend. I smiled sleepily at Fenella, who said she must leave. She refused the offer of the spare room. She said she would ring me tomorrow. It was Saturday, known to be a very low time when people were unhappy.

As I drifted off into the first proper sleep I had known for months, I remembered that she didn't have my telephone number. Well, maybe I could find her again, I thought; Fenella can't be a very usual name. I couldn't think what her last name was, or what she did for a living, or where she lived. She must have told me. Surely? We couldn't have talked about ME all that time. But sleep was stronger than puzzlement. I didn't even turn off the light.

I was on my second cup of coffee when she rang. She

had taken down the number, she said; I was too distressed
to be bothered with trivialities. Would we go to the park?
It was such a lovely day. We could walk and talk without
anyone disturbing us. I felt a little twinge that surely I
had talked enough, but she seemed so caring it would
almost have been throwing her friendship back in her
face. And indeed that sunny day while lovers entwined
and mothers talked between screaming for toddlers, when
old men read newspapers and told each other about things
that had happened years ago, Fenella and I walked the
length and the breadth of one of London's big parks. And
sometimes we sat, and she had brought small sandwiches
and a flask of coffee so that we didn't have to leave until
my legs were tired and my eyes were aching for all the
tears they had wept as I told her of the first night with
John, and of how he had always loved me even before
Maria had gone to this clairvoyante which had tilted her
mind and sent her in search of unsuitable love and un-
reachable dreams. I told her trivia too, of how John and
I used to play Animal Snap in bed and how we used to
do Tommy Cooper imitations with little hats like a fez.

Fenella remembered everything. Every single thing.

'It must have been hard for you both when Maria took
up all this card business herself. You know, dealing and
redealing,' she said.

I had forgotten that I had told her about Maria and the
Tarot cards.

By Sunday I felt strong enough to go and see John, this
time without making a scene. I had known two good
nights' sleep. I had talked out every heartbeat of the thing.
There would be no emotion, no drama, no terrible
recriminations.

On the way back from John's house, through the blurry
tears I wondered what kind of self-absorption had allowed

me to let Fenella go without asking her where she lived, or for her phone number.

But when I got to my flat she was sitting in the court-yard. It was a warm evening and she sat calmly unhurried on one of the rather folksy carved benches under the old cherry tree.

'I thought you might need me,' she said.

'You must think I'm very weak,' I sobbed as I sat on my bed drinking the honey, lemon and hot water which she said was soothing. Fenella sat in a chair.

'Was this where you dressed up in your fez to play Animal Snap?' she asked, and I was so godamned touched she remembered that I cried all over again.

She was so good to me, Fenella was, she had all the time in the world. Of course I did take her address and her phone number, and found out that she worked in a rights agency. It sounded fascinating, but Fenella didn't talk much about it; she said she didn't want to bore me with the technicalities of her job. They just acted as brokers between literary agents in Britain and on the continent. They suggested books that might be translated into Greek or Italian or whatever, and they got a commission on them. Did she meet a lot of fascinating people I wondered? Not many, they didn't deal with the authors directly you see. I saw, and asked little more about Fenella's job. Because I talked so much about my own.

I told her what stick-in-the-muds they were and how they never tried to set up anything new for the children in the school. How I longed to invite authors in to tell them what it was REALLY like to write. To let them meet living writers instead of assuming that anyone who wrote was long buried. I had been hoping for the woman who wrote *Open Windows*. Not really a children's book, of course, but surprising how many of the Sixth Form had read it and identified with the rage against mothers that went through it. But I had not been able to find out where the author lived and was sure that the publishers might never forward a letter, especially if it was a speaking request.

'I can give you her address,' Fenella said, surprisingly. It turned out that they had handled deals for the translations and European sales.

'Is she nice?' I couldn't believe that anyone knew her.

'I used to know her quite well when her mother had a horrible hip injury, we talked a lot in those days. But she's too busy to chat now.' Fenella's voice was cold.

She was not too busy, however, to come to the school. And they liked her enormously. She didn't talk down to them. She said, quite truthfully, that she did have a dreadful mother herself, but then so did most people including her own children. They liked that; it made them think. It made me think too. I thought about my own mother, long dead now in Ireland. I had never visited her grave. Did that make me a dreadful daughter? She had been a dreadful mother in ways, wanting me to live at home in the country and marry a man who owned a pub. She said it was Fast to travel as I did, that no man would want me. Perhaps she had been right after all. I talked about it for hours with Fenella.

The children wanted Louise Mitchell too, the one that writes those so-called historical sagas. For once I saw eye to eye with the Principal, that they were in fact pornography. I wondered – was I becoming more conservative or was the Principal becoming more aware of the world? We did have Maxwell Lawrie at the school, the creator of Vladimir Klein. He was marvellous with children, told them how to write spy books and thrillers by beginning on the last page and working it out from there. It was like a problem, he said; just see who couldn't have done it and eliminate them, and then find an improbable motive for the one who could have done it and start at the beginning.

He stayed for coffee in the staff room and he seemed to be giving me the eye a bit. Said that he'd like ten children at least. Wouldn't I? I said yes, I agreed totally, might as well have a brood; they'd be company for each other and more fun, but if we were going to do it we'd better set about it fairly soon. He suggested that night. I think he was ninety per cent joking. Fenella said he was sick, and it would have been madness to get involved before my wounds were healed. It was funny, that was when I realised that my wounds had healed. I rarely thought of John now, and that Maxwell Lawrie . . . which wasn't his real name at all – he was Cyril Biggs . . . he did seem interesting. I didn't think his approach was sick, I thought it was jokey. It was just a way of speaking. I mean, I'm twenty-eight; he is a great deal more. You don't say things like would you come on a date with me when you get to our stage, do you? You make jokes about having to start soon to create ten people or what-ever. Fenella's lips were pursed. I let it go. She was so nice and generous I didn't want to upset her.

Cyril had told me that we should have Mavis Ormitage to talk at the school. A wonderful woman, he said. She is enormous, wears white just to make herself look a little larger still. People used to call her Moby Dick, She wrote true romances, hundreds of them. Cyril knew her because they met every summer at a Writer's School. She had a real gift for talking about Life, made it all seem quite simple and easy to handle somehow, and a great laugh like a roll of drums to go with it. I had thought that the Principal mightn't go for 'the Queen of the Trues' as she was called. Cyril said he'd have a word; it was easy to make a superficial decision without meeting the person. Mavis would be good for those kids about to set out on Life; she knew it all somehow without being preachy. That's why she was such a success. She drove around everywhere in a Landrover, wearing a white raincoat and white lifeboatman's hat when it rained. She kept her books in plastic bags because she liked open cars and the feel of rain on her face. That sort of thing had to be helpful to children, Cyril said.

Fenella knew Mavis Ormitage. I couldn't believe it! In a city of twelve million people she had known two people that I had come across too. And Mavis wasn't even a client. Fenella said that there was no way HER sort of writing would translate; it was amazing enough that it sold here.

No, Fenella had met Mavis Ormitage in real life, oh, it must be about five years ago now. She had a daughter who was totally incapacitated and she had given her life to this girl. Well, she wasn't a girl, she was a woman; the daughter must have been in her forties when she had been driven to put her into a hospital. Fenella had a friend, Ruth, who worked in the hospital.

I had never heard of Ruth.

'Where is she now? Ruth, I mean.' Fenella had no idea. Ruth had been very depressed in those days; she had this really diabolical mother. Talk of the mother in *Open Windows*! This one dressed like a teenager and was totally pathetic, going around groping men in the street. Poor Ruth had been very low indeed, but in order to drag herself out of it she had taken up voluntary work in the hospital. And by chance Ruth had been to a writers' course that Mavis Ormitage had been lecturing at, must have been the same one as that Cyril.

I felt Fenella disapproved of 'that Cyril'. And Mavis. And, in some way, her friend Ruth.

Anyway, it was all very briefly told: Fenella didn't ever go into much detail about herself. But Mavis recognised Ruth who was working taking round trolleys of books and magazines. They all used to talk in the hospital corridors, and in the canteen and in the nice big garden of the hospital. I could see it very well: Fenella finding the right seats and the right tree to overhang them, Mavis talking about her dying daughter and Ruth telling of the mad, groping mother.

Both of them leaning on Fenella's interest, her phenomenal memory for the minutiae of their stories.

'Those were good days,' Fenella said. 'We had good conversations under a tree in the hospital garden.' Her face looked far away as she thought of the good days, when she heard about the grossness of a mad old woman and the slow, lingering death of a bloated handicapped girl.

I felt a shiver and wished that I had gone out with Cyril Biggs that night.

It wasn't a question of procreating ten, or indeed any children. He was a funny, self-deprecating kind of man, who didn't take himself or anyone else seriously. Had I told him about John and Maria, which would have been highly unlikely, he would have dismissed it briefly. He would not have asked what Maria said when she first found out about John and how we had betrayed her.

Mavis Ormitage was undoubtedly the most talked-of visitor the school had ever known. From the moment she roared up the drive in her open Landrover and stepped, in billowing silk, into the school hall they loved her. She demanded questions afterwards and only when the school security men said it was time to lock the gates could she be prised away.

Mavis Ormitage had a small brandy flask and she topped up everyone's coffee in the Staff room. Even the Principal seemed enthusiastic about the celebration, something that had never been known. I brought myself to mention Fenella. It wasn't easy. For two reasons: it was hard to get Mavis alone for one thing and also I was almost afraid that it was disloyal. It was like probing a sore tooth: ask about Fenella and I will hear something bad. Why do I want to hear something bad about a woman who has been so kind to me? Am I looking for an excuse to stop seeing her?

Mavis had small beady eyes in the middle of all the creases of good-humoured flesh.

'One of the kindest people I ever met,' Mavis said, 'at the time. There's a time for Fenella like the old Psalm says; there's a time for being born, and dying, and for Fenella.'

'And when the time is over?' I asked.

'You'll know, but Fenella will never know. She is like a doomed ship, always encountering other stricken ships, helping them and then being abandoned by them.'

It was a bit flowery, and it also made me feel guilty. I was feeling better now. I didn't WANT to talk about John and Maria or not having visited my mother's grave or sleepless nights or uncaring colleagues. Things were looking up. Only Fenella was looking down.

'What happened to Ruth?' I wanted to know.

'Marvellous things,' said Mavis, wobbling with pleasure. 'Her mother got heavily involved with three handsome young Jewish grocers, nobody knows which if any of them is her lover. She has calmed down totally and is a businesswoman extraordinary. Ruth met this wonderful man who works in the museum; they're doing that big Dinosaur Exhibit, you know, the one that's getting all the publicity?'

'But they're getting married. I saw it in the papers,' I cried, excitedly. 'They're going to have the ceremony in the Prehistoric Hall.'

'She invited Fenella but she knows she won't get an answer.'

There was a little silence.

I had to speak quickly lest someone took marvellous Mavis Ormitage away from me.

'Was it when you got better, you know, stopped being a stricken ship that you felt it a bit. . . .'

'She was a wonderful person for her time,' Mavis repeated.

'Will I give her your love, say you were asking for her?' I knew it was a hollow kind of thing.

'No, no. Wiser not. Anyway the ocean is full of stricken ships, you'll discover that later . . . I mean, before me there was that marvellous woman who wrote *Open Windows* who had that devil of a mother, and then there was Ruth, and then there was me, and between me and you there were plenty.'

A few weeks later when I used to leap at the ring of the phone and hope it was Cyril again, my heart was leaden when it was Fenella.

'Oppressive day today, I suppose it's brought you down,' she would say.

I remembered something Mavis Ormitage said. She had been talking to the Principal about her answering machine.

'No, no, it's not because I get lots of calls, most people don't know where I am. I bought it a while ago to preserve my good humour. You can't get brought down by a machine like you can by a voice. A voice whose time is past.'

The Principal had nodded vaguely and confusedly, unaccustomed to the tot of brandy in the coffee. But I knew now what Mavis had meant. And anyway Cyril said he loved leaving messages on machines. It made him feel inventive, creative, and even, when the mood called for it, it made him feel loving.

The Fish-Sitter

RUTH RENDELL

Since her first novel, *From Doon with Death*, was published in 1964, Ruth Rendell has won many awards, including the Crime Writers' Association Gold Dagger for 1976's best crime novel with *A Demon in my View* and the Arts Council National Book Award – Genre Fiction for *Lake of Darkness* in 1980. In 1984 Ruth Rendell won her second Edgar from the Mystery Writers of America for best short story with 'The New Girl Friend', and in 1985 received the Silver Dagger for *The Tree of Hands*. In 1966 she won another Edgar for *A Dark-Adapted Eye*, written under the pseudonym of Barbara Vine, and in the same month was awarded a Gold Dagger for *Live Flesh*. Her books have been translated into fifteen languages and are also published to great acclaim in the United States. Ruth Rendell is married and lives in a sixteenth-century farmhouse in Suffolk.

THE FISH-SITTER

Next door to the Empress Court Disco Roller Rink in Seoul Road, Southend was the south-east Essex branch of Daleth Foods and next to that the Aquarium. It was a parade of interesting and even exotic emporia such as are often found in the hinterland of seaside resorts. Goods were sold, services offered and entertainment provided. For instance, in a flatlet above Magda's Sports Equipment Ruth Church the clairvoyante, lately known as Ruta Yglesias, told fortunes, and at the photographer's, last in the parade, little girls might dress up in tutus with ribbon laces cross-gartered to their knees and dream as they posed that they were Veronica Spencer dancing *Giselle*.

The Aquarium's real name was Malvina's Marine Museum, a grand title for what was quite a modest affair. On a sunny afternoon, when the beaches were crowded and the Ruler, ever-measuring, assessed the candy floss queue at one thousand three hundred metres long, Mrs Trevor was showing her fish-sitter round the tank room.

It was lit, even on a day like this, for each tank had its own light as well as its own aeration pump. These were necessarily at floor-level, set to illuminate the green ever-moving, ever-bubbling water below, and sending up into the tank room a glaucous, rather misty, glow. In the room below, visitors to the Aquarium could be seen only occasionally and then dimly through glass and water as they moved, mostly in silence, between the Sarcopterygii, the Selachii and the Decapoda. Some paused to read the printed and illustrated labels attached to the wall by each tank. Others pressed their faces against the cool glass and the marine creatures swam close to inspect them.

'Do you know, Cyril, this will be the first holiday I've had since I started this place,' Mrs Trevor was saying. 'Well, come to that, the first since I stopped working for you-know-who.'

Cyril knew very well who and was no more anxious to speak the name of the famous romantic novelist than was her erstwhile home help. This attitude, on both their parts, brought him a pang of guilt, for would he have ever known Mrs Trevor but for Louise Mitchell? This job, this temporary roof over his head, would certainly not have come about without her. Gazing down at the decapod among the weeds and branched coral below, he subtly changed the subject.

'I wonder that you chose to go on a Caribbean cruise, though. Won't it be rather a case of coals to Newcastle?'

'What very unfortunate and hackneyed metaphors you do pick on, Cyril,' said Mrs Trevor sharply. 'You always have. What do you know about cruises, anyway?'

A meek man, or one who had that reputation, Cyril only smiled. He could have said something about the days of his employment on a cruise ship but he did not, though as he watched the crab's sideways progress among darting jewel-bright chimaera he remembered the flying fish which had pursued the ship and his friend who supervised the ladies' cloakroom next door with her collection of newts she called salamanders. He also recalled the food on the *Cybele*, the leavings of which had come his way and hers.

'The green-carapaced crab,' he said dreamily, 'whose meat is sweet to eat.'

'None of that, please. Part of my pleasure in running this place is in knowing these innocent creatures are safe from the fisherman's net and the treacherous lobster pot. You don't eat fish, do you, Cyril?'

'Not this sort at any rate,' said Cyril, his eyes now on some variety of many-tentacled octopus or squid. 'Why does nothing live in the biggest tank?'

'I'm hoping to acquire a shark,' said Mrs Trevor. 'Possibly even Carcharhinus milberti. Now you know what you have to do, don't you, Cyril? You close at five and then you come up here and feed the innocent creatures. Specific feeding instructions are all in the book. You turn off the lights but *not* the aeration and in certain cases cover the tanks with their lids. Is that understood?

Cyril said it was and what about cleaning out the tanks? Some, he had noticed, were much overgrown with green algae which had even covered the back of the stone crab.

'Carlos will come in and do that. It's a specialist job. You're the kind of person who would use Persil Automatic.'

He knew she was angry with him for what he had said about crabmeat and not for the first time castigated himself for his tactless ways. They went downstairs and Mrs Trevor resumed her seat behind the ticket window so that Shana from the rink could get back to her duties. Cyril, in the cosy sitting room at the rear of the Aquarium, found his instruction book *The Care of Cold-Blooded Aquatic Vertebra and Crustaceae* on a shelf between *Story and Structure* and Louise's novel *Open Windows*. But he did not read it, he looked unseeing at the pages.

As usual in one of his reveries, he trudged across familiar ground. Biggs was not such a bad name. It was an improvement on Smalls, for instance, with its connotations of underclothes. Several saints had been called Cyril. He had looked them up in encyclopaedias. There were Saint Cyril of Jerusalem and Saint Cyril of Alexandria, both Doctors of the Church. There was that Saint Cyril who was responsible for christianising the Danubian Slavs, and who invented the Cyrillic writing system. It is not everyone who can boast of sharing his name with an alphabet.

Was it his name which had doomed him to obscurity, and worse, to mockery? People laughed when they heard he was an insurance claims inspector, as if someone called that could hardly be anything else. But his venture at changing his name and adopting another profession had met with disaster. 'Maxwell Lawrie' sounded distinguished. For a time his books featuring Vladimir Klein, international espionage agent, had brought him success and promised fame. *Glasnost* had put an end to all hope there, for who cares for spies when there may soon be nothing and no-one left to spy on?

You cannot get back into insurance when you have been absent from it for so long, but Cyril had not even tried. Before he came back to Southend and Malvina's Marine Museum, he had been living on alms given him by the Espionage Authors' Benevolent Association in a hotel room in Madagascar Road, NW2, paid for by Brent Council. There he had often sat and wondered what might be the destiny of one called Cyril Biggs. Surely there must be more than to be the prototype of the dull little man in the novel, the one with thinning hair and the ugly wife, the one with shoes always dull with the dust of mean streets. He sensed sometimes that he had never had his full potential realised, though he did know what that potential might be.

Malvina Trevor left for Southampton as soon as the Aquarium closed. She had dressed herself in a grey-green suit with a frilly blouse. Once her taxi had disappeared round the corner of Seoul Road, Cyril went up to the tank room and carefully scattered fish food into the tanks. He switched off the lights, but not the aeration and heating plant, and where instructed closed the lids. It was a complex routine which, once learned, became simple. Day after day it was repeated. From ten till five Cyril sat at the ticket window. At five-thirty he fed the fish and closed up the tank room. On two days a week Shana came in to relieve him and several times Ruta Yglesias asked him in to supper.

Louise Mitchell was there on one occasion, for the sisters had always been close, and their mother with them. On another Ruta had invited some people called Ann and Roger, whose surname Cyril no more learned than he did the christian name of another guest, Mrs Greenaway. But it was quite a party and, to his surprise, Cyril enjoyed himself. He was not really gloomy by nature, only shy and lacking confidence. Before Malvina returned, and she would be back in less than a week, Cyril made up his mind to return Ruta's hospitality.

Giving dinner parties was not something he was accustomed to. For days he agonised over what he should give Ruta, Mrs Church and Mavis Ormitage to eat. With Shana ensconced behind the ticket window, he roved the front at Southend, eyeing the fish stalls, and in equal doubt and confusion paced between the freezers in the Presto supermarket. Food was expensive, or that kind was. The price of crabs and lobsters horrified him. He informed the stone crab in the Aquarium of the amount asked for its fellows when 'dressed' and offered for sale on the stalls. The crab's reply was to scamper sideways across its weedy coralline floor. I wonder if it is really green-carapaced, thought Cyril, or if its back is the reddy-pink colour of those I saw this afternoon. It is hard to tell because of the algae which cover it.

The main course was to be pasta, the kind the Italians call *alle vongole* because it has small scallops mixed up in it. Cyril bought the pasta at Daleth Foods but naturally the Orthodox Jews who ran it would have nothing to do with seafood. The shellfish came from his favourite stall on the front – it was the cheapest – where he also bought a large dressed crab. Cyril mixed its sweet meat with Hellmann's mayonnaise to make it go further and everyone pronounced it delicious. But when Mavis made a remark about its being rather strange to eat shellfish with 'all that lot swimming about in there', he felt uncomfortable. Had he been wrong to choose this menu? Had he made himself look a fool?

'Does that mean zoo keepers must be vegetarians then, Mavis? asked Mrs Church.

Mavis giggled. 'You know what I mean. If you had supper with a zoo keeper you wouldn't imagine you were eating lion chops but here – well, you know what I mean.'

They all did and Cyril could not help noticing that Ruta left a great many of her *vongole* on the side of her plate. What had induced him to make a lime mousse in a fish shape for pudding? It must have been seeing the copper mould in the window of the shop at the end of the parade where Mr Cybele sold antique scoops. Mr Cybele had lent him the fish mould and the pale green shape looked pretty. Unfortunately no-one wanted to eat it after what Mavis Ormitage had said.

Cyril felt that his party had been a failure. That, of

course, was nothing new. Most of his ventures, large and small, were failures. The arrival in the morning of Carlos with his tank-cleaning equipment distracted his mind from unhappy reminiscing. Cyril hung a notice on the Aquarium door, announcing that it would be closed till after lunch. He inspected the tanks before reopening. The improvement in their appearance was quite wonderful. Everything sparkled, fresh and gleaming. Every aquatic vertebra looked rejuvenated – except the stone crab whose carapace was still overgrown with dense green fur.

Its appearance troubled him. When he went about his feeding routine he put one finger into the water, touched the shell and found he could easily scrape some of the crust of algae off with his fingernail. Carlos had cleaned the biggest tank in the middle of the room as well and Cyril, closing the lid on the crab, wondered when the new shark would arrive. Before Malvina's return or after? She was coming back in two days' time. Ruta and Mrs Church were driving to Southampton in Mrs Church's new Audi to fetch her.

Cyril slept badly that night. He saw himself as a social misfit. He wondered about his future, which seemed to have no existence beyond Malvina's return. A great crowd came to the Aquarium in the morning and entrance had to be restricted. Visitors had heard about the cleaning operation and for the first time Cyril saw a queue at the front door. When the last visitor had left at five he paced up and down the sitting room, uncertain what to do, torn by conflicting demands. Then, impulsively, he rushed upstairs. He lifted the large, algae-coated decapod out of its tank, took it to the bathroom and washed it under the running tap. It was the work of a moment. The crab's carapace was indeed green, a pure soft emerald green with a curious design like an ideograph in a dark purplish shade on its back.

Tenderly, Cyril restored it to its home. The crab scuttled through its woodland of weed across its coral floor, attended by a little shoal of fish coloured like jewels. If Malvina enquired, he decided, he would tell her it had somehow happened during Carlos's operations. But surely she would be delighted? Cyril suddenly found himself hyper-anxious to please Malvina, to confront her with perfection, to have attained, so to speak, supererogatory heights of achievement. Merely to have done the appointed job was not enough. He spent most of Saturday night sweeping and vacuum-cleaning Aquarium, tank room and the rest of the house, and on Sunday morning wrote in his best lettering a label for the biggest tank: Carcharhinus milberti, the Sandbar Shark, which he followed by a careful description of its habitat and habits.

Mrs Trevor came back at seven in the evening, dressed exactly as she had been when she left. She entered the Aquarium alone and trembling with anger. Cyril had expected Ruta and Mrs Church to be with her but evidently they had thought it wisest to make themselves scarce. Malvina gave each tank a rapid, penetrating glance, the stone crab a longer look. She went upstairs and Cyril followed. So far she had not uttered a word and Cyril had received no reply to his enquiries as to her health and enjoyment of her trip. In the tank room she stood looking down at the stone crab, turned to face Cyril and said in shrill tones,

'How dare you?'

Putting the blame on Carlos forgotten, Cyril stammered that the crab was not harmed, indeed seemed happier for the cleaning operation.

'Don't give me that. Don't even think of trying it. I

know what you have done. Ruta and her mother told me all about the seafood extravaganza you served up to them – and the ingredients used. This particular decapod, I have no doubt, was purchased or stolen from the tank of one of the fish restaurants on the front. Monterroso's, most probably.'

'It isn't true, Malvina. They're lying. I wouldn't do that.'

'I'm not a fool, you know. It isn't even the same variety. Look at the colour! You're too ignorant to know that there are no less than 4,500 hundred species of crab, aren't you? You thought, when you slaughtered that innocent creature to make mayonnaise, that one crab was very like another. Well, I shall expose you. I shall publish the whole story in the *Southend Times*. Needless to say, I shan't pay you. I shall not take you on as my permanent assistant, as was in my mind.'

Cyril did not think. He did not hesitate. He gave her a shove and she fell into the biggest tank with a scream and a loud splash. If he saw her floundering there, he might soften, he thought, for he had never been hardhearted, so he put the lid on, went downstairs and out to the beach. In all his life he had never felt so happy, so free and so fulfilled. As he walked along the mudflats with the sea breezes in his hair, he understood his destiny and the meaning of his name.

He was not a novelist's character, no figment of fiction, but one to inspire literature in his own right. One day books would be written about him, his past, his history, his obscurity, his striving for an identity, and his name: Cyril Biggs, the Marine Museum Murderer. Newspapers would give him headlines and television a favoured position in the six o'clock news. At Madame Tussaud's, in the Chamber of Horrors, he would be placed by a water tank while a plastic facsimile of his victim floated within. He had found his vocation.

That night Cyril slept better than he had done for years. It was Shana's day to sit at the receipt of custom. Such news travels fast and, looking out of an upstairs window, Cyril was not surprised to see a queue winding its way from the front door the length of the parade. Presently he crept down to the tank room.

He did not lift the lid from the biggest tank but edged discreetly along the wall and peered into the stone crab's home, peered through sparkling, ever-bubbling jade-coloured water and gleaming, spotless glass to the crowds beneath. There, pressed closely around the biggest tank were Louise Mitchell, Ruta Yglesias, Fenella, Mrs Church and Mrs Greenaway, Henry Bennett with the Ruler and his painted queen, the three Jewish grocers, Veronica Spencer and her husband Tim, Margaret Cavendish, Jane, several Italian boys in T-shirts and a host of others not recognisable to Cyril. Some were reading the label he had made for the Sandbar shark but those who could get close had their faces pressed against the glass, contemplating what was within.

They were polite middle-class people and as each had seen her or his fill, there was a stepping back and a parting to allow those behind to look. In one of these reshuffles, the tank was briefly revealed to Cyril's view and he saw floating inside it, flippers gently pulsating with the movement of the water, a vast grey-green shape with a frill about its neck like the ruff of a salamander.

SUBSCRIBE TO STORIA

For just £10 you can read the latest and very best short stories over the next year.

STORIA 4, due out in the spring, 1990, will be GREEN and includes work by Sue Townsend, Deborah Levy, Candia McWilliam, Maggie Gee and Sara Maitland.

Just send a cheque for £10 made payable to Pandora Press (add £4 postage and packing if outside the UK) and two issues of STORIA will be sent to your home.

Pandora Press
15–17 BROADWICK STREET
LONDON W1V 1FP

STORIA 1

DYAN SHELDON
MIRIAM TLALI
KATE PULLINGER
ANN ZIETY
JEANETTE WINTERSON
ANNE MCMANUS
LINDA ANDERSON
KATHY ACKER
FAY WELDON
SARAH BAYLIS

MICHELENE WANDOR
MARIANNE WIGGINS
HANAN AL SHAYKH
JANET FRAME
HELEN SIMPSON
JOAN RILEY
RUTH RENDELL
DAPHNE DU MAURIER

0-04-440276-7

STORIA 2
LOVE

Love is an obsession, an ambition, a delicious and essential source of food and warmth at its best and a trigger for lasting trauma at its worst. In the second issue of Pandora's vibrant new fiction magazine, contemporary writers look at love, at what happens when a young girl answers a lonely hearts advertisement and finds a sadist at the other end, at the pointless and self destructive way that women wait for men, at the speed love can turn to hate and at the generosity and depth of people who can love and appreciate others for who they really are.

EMMA TENNANT
REBECCA BROWN
KATHLEEN STEWART
MARY ROBISON
ALICE ADAMS
ANNA FRIEND
TAMA JANOWITZ
CAROL RUMENS
RUTH RENDELL
MARY FLANAGAN

JOAN SMITH
NOELE MACKNESS
HANAN AL SHAYKH
A. S. BYATT
HELEN SIMPSON
LISA ST AUBIN DE TERAN
JAYNE ANNE PHILIPS
ANNE LEATON

0-04-440355-0